"Eve, there ███████ **exist, you a** ███████ **us."**

Ethan said it softly because the baby in his arms seemed to be drifting off.

"I obviously can't do this. Last night was proof."

"Last night meant nothing. You've always managed, Eve. You're strong and you're capable."

"Before, Ethan," she said sadly. "I was that person before. This is me now."

"I guess you have changed. I've never heard you say you can't."

He glanced down at the little girl in his arms. "What other option is there? Should we turn her over to the state, let her take her chances with whoever they choose? Find some distant relative?"

Ethan leaned back in the chair and studied Eve's face. She was everything familiar. His childhood friend. The person he'd loved. She looked as stubborn as ever. But there was something fragile in her expression. Something that made him recheck his feelings. Eve had been his only broken heart. He didn't want another one…

Brenda Minton lives in the Ozarks with her husband, children, cats, dogs and strays. She is a pastor's wife, Sunday-school teacher, coffee addict and sleep deprived. Not in that order. Her dream to be an author for Harlequin started somewhere in the pages of a romance novel about a young American woman stranded in a Spanish castle. Her dreams came true, and twenty-plus books later, she is an author hoping to inspire young girls to dream.

Books by Brenda Minton

Love Inspired

Mercy Ranch

Reunited with the Rancher
The Rancher's Christmas Match
Her Oklahoma Rancher

Bluebonnet Springs

Second Chance Rancher
The Rancher's Christmas Bride
The Rancher's Secret Child

Martin's Crossing

A Rancher for Christmas
The Rancher Takes a Bride
The Rancher's Second Chance
The Rancher's First Love
Her Rancher Bodyguard
Her Guardian Rancher

Visit the Author Profile page at Harlequin.com for more titles.

Her Oklahoma Rancher

Brenda Minton

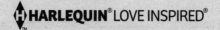

LOVE INSPIRED BOOKS

Recycling programs
for this product may
not exist in your area.

ISBN-13: 978-1-335-47920-4

Her Oklahoma Rancher

www.Harlequin.com

Printed in U.S.A.

And we know that all things work together for good to them that love God, to them who are the called according to his purpose.
—*Romans* 8:28

This book is dedicated to my agent, Melissa Jeglinski, for guiding me through this process. She puts up with my angst, cheers me on and encourages me. Thank you!

Chapter One

Four years ago Hope, Oklahoma, had been a forgotten lake town, and Eve Vincent had been a patient in a VA hospital coming to terms with her new reality. As she transferred from her car to the wheelchair next to it, she realized that they'd both changed. The town was booming again. The resorts and hotels were up and running, and stores were reopened with new businesses. And Eve, like the little town of Hope, had reinvented herself. She'd survived the changes that had happened after an IED exploded, leaving her paralyzed from the waist down.

Eve hadn't grown up in Hope but she now considered the little town her home. She had moved here to live on Mercy Ranch, owned by Jack West, the same man who had infused money and time into the local economy, essentially reviving the town. What Jack had done for Hope, he'd also done for the wounded warriors he'd brought to his ranch. He'd given them all a second chance and a way to start over.

Sometimes she thought about going back home to

Texas. But home was too complicated. Her aging parents would want to coddle her even as they reminded her they had begged her not to join the army. Going back to Texas would mean facing the past, facing memories and people. The past was best left in the past. She had a new life, a new reality. Tough as it had been, she'd found happiness here. Contentment even.

As she headed for the ramp at the side of Mattie's Café, she raised her face to the warm, late April sunshine. A perfect day. She glanced around, searching for Kylie West's car. They met every Monday for lunch. It had been their routine since Kylie married Jack West's son, Carson.

Kylie met her at the top of the ramp, holding the door open for Eve to enter the café. Eve smiled up at her friend. Kylie held her two-month-old foster daughter in her arms and she looked every bit the happy wife and mother she should be.

"You beat me here. Even with a baby and two kids, you're early," Eve teased her friend. Kylie was always early.

"It's a hard habit to break," Kylie said as she followed Eve into the diner. "I have a table in the corner."

"Perfect."

Holly, the owner of Mattie's, approached with water and menus. She looked frazzled, her dark hair in a messy bun and circles under her eyes that suggested she hadn't been sleeping.

"You okay, Holly?" Eve asked as the other woman set glasses of water on the table.

"It's been a busy morning. Hectic. And, you know, life."

"Anything we can do?" Kylie asked.

Holly shook her head but Eve thought she saw moisture gather in her eyes. "Nope. I've got this. I'll be right back to get your orders."

"I wish she understood that she has friends who are willing to help her." Kylie situated her infant daughter in Eve's arms. "I'm guessing that, even though you don't like kids, babies or kittens, you want to hold this little darling?"

"I'm not *that* horrible." Eve gladly took the tiny little girl. "I like kittens."

"You're absolutely not horrible," Kylie assured her.

"And I think Holly is just holding everything together and afraid if she cracks, even a little, the dam will burst."

"Agreed."

Eve's phone rang. Kylie reached for her purse but Eve stopped her. "No. It's probably my parents. And I don't want to talk to them."

"You're not talking to them?"

"Today you're my friend, not my therapist." Eve kissed the downy head of the infant in her arms. "I love this precious nugget."

"Do not call her a nugget."

"She's bite-sized." She kissed Cara's cheeks and was rewarded with the sweetest baby smile. Brown eyes focused on Eve's face and another grin followed.

"She's beautiful, isn't she?" Kylie asked with a dreamy voice.

"Are you seriously asking that question? Of course she's beautiful." Eve sighed as she held the baby close, sniffing hair that smelled of lavender.

She wanted one. She wouldn't admit it, even to her best friend. Half the time she couldn't even admit it to herself. She wanted what she couldn't have. A husband, a family, a home of her own. Instead of admitting to those secret things, she smiled.

She shook her head slightly, dislodging the hint of melancholy. She was happy. She loved her life at Mercy Ranch. She loved her life. Period. She had a job translating documents and manuals to English. Four years ago she hadn't dreamed she would be able to resume her life to this degree, so of course she was happy. The military had sent her to language school and she could still use those hard earned skills to support herself.

Her phone rang again. She held Cara in her right arm and reached for the phone with her left. The caller seemed to be getting smarter in their attempts to reach her. This time the number was blocked. She thought of friends she'd ultimately blocked from her life, lost contact with, pushed aside. All because she hadn't wanted to face them from this chair. She hadn't wanted to face their pity.

When she looked up, Kylie was watching, compassion in her eyes.

"Your parents again?" Kylie asked.

"No caller ID so I doubt it. Our last phone call didn't end well and I told them I needed space but they've never blocked their number before."

"Friend or therapist, I'm going to give you some advice." Kylie moved her chair close. "You have to deal with your parents. They love you and you love them. Tell them what you need from them."

"I know I'm going to have to talk to them, face-to-face. But somehow I have to make them see that I can't come home. Mercy Ranch is my home now." She focused on the baby in her arms. "They would chip away at my faith, my independence. I just can't."

The bell over the front door clanged. Eve glanced that way. Nothing unusual, a stranger walking through the doors of the café. It happened more frequently these days. Jack's plan to bring tourists back to Hope had been successful. She started to glance away but the man walking through the door with a baby in his arms wasn't a stranger. Suddenly she felt her skin go cold and her ears buzzed.

"Eve, are you okay?" Kylie swooped in to take her baby. "Breathe."

"I can't… I can't breathe. I have to leave. I need to get out of here."

Kylie followed her gaze toward the front of the café and the man standing just inside the door. He zeroed in on Eve with lightning precision. Eve reached for her glass of water, hands trembling as she lifted it to her lips.

"Who is he?" Kylie asked.

"Her worst nightmare," he said as he approached their table.

Holly chose that moment to appear.

"Do I need to bring another menu?" she asked.

"Yes," he said. At the same time Eve shook her head and said, "No."

Holly looked to Eve. She didn't know how to get the words out. She didn't know what to say. Her past, present and future had just collided in one big messy pileup and her heart still couldn't catch up.

Six years since they'd seen each other. Six years and he still had the ability to undo everything inside her. She couldn't let him do that to her. She drew in a deep breath, ignored his dark auburn hair, the strength of his chin, the deep brown of his eyes. Okay, she didn't really ignore anything about him. How could she when he was looming over her?

With a baby.

"Ethan, what are you doing here?" Her voice came out in a squeak.

"Obviously I'm finding out some things I didn't know." His voice changed from harsh to questioning, hurt maybe?

"Why don't you have a seat?" Kylie offered, pulling up another chair. "Your baby is beautiful."

He looked down at the bundle in his arms, as if he'd forgotten about the baby in the pink dress, all soft blond hair and big eyes.

Kylie looked from the baby to Eve. A baby. Eve shouldn't be surprised. Four years of silence meant that any number of things could have happened in Ethan's life. Including a wife and children. But what was he doing here? Why now?

She waited, knowing that whatever Ethan had to say, it would hurt. And it would change her life. She felt the devastation coming and couldn't do a thing to stop it. Without thinking she grabbed Kylie's hand, needing strength from her best friend as the man sitting at their table stared her down, accusations and pain shining in his dark eyes.

For several years Ethan Forester had run the scenarios through his mind, trying to decide which one best fit Eve's defection from his life, from the life they'd planned together. In his mind the phone call ending their engagement had been made because she'd found someone else or possibly decided she wanted a military career over a marriage to a rancher from Texas. Her parents had never been in favor of their relationship so maybe she'd come around to their way of thinking. That's what he'd told himself. It hadn't made him feel any better but it had helped him to deal with the loss.

Even with the possible explanations, he'd struggled with how they'd gone from in love and engaged to separated and never seeing one another again. Over the phone they'd been planning the wedding because she would have been leaving the army and coming home. They'd picked the venue, the caterer, had even discussed bridesmaids and groomsmen. And then silence for several months.

Their next phone call had been her telling him their engagement was over and that she never wanted to see him again. Her parents had refused to tell him anything. No surprises there.

Now, face-to-face with her, he got it. And he was angry and hurt all over again. After years of being best friends, in love, engaged, she had kept this from him.

"You could have told me about…" The words came out, torn from somewhere deep inside. "You could have trusted me enough to tell me."

"Not here," she said. She turned away from him, not before he saw the flash of pain that flickered in her brown eyes.

He didn't want to feel her pain. The moment sympathy tried to surface, he shoved it back down. Tori shifted in his arms and hugged his neck, a reminder that this wasn't about him. It wasn't about Eve. The six-month-old in his arms came first. This was about her life, her future.

He'd had the most difficult two weeks of his life. Tori had shared in the devastation. She was just too young to really understand how her life had changed on a rainy night two weeks ago.

The devastation he'd felt was about to be visited on the woman sitting in front of him, dark eyes warily studying the child in his arms.

"You're right. Not here." He didn't know how to proceed. "Where can we talk?"

She backed away from the table, her gaze flicking briefly to the woman sitting across from her. She noticed his attention on that woman and she sighed.

"Ethan Forester, this is my friend Kylie West and her daughter Cara." Her gaze shot to the child in his arms.

A child she might have known had she kept in contact with friends. He should give her a definition of the word, so she would understand what it meant to her family, to her friends, that she'd disappeared from their lives.

Kylie gave him an easy smile. "There's a small, private room through the door at the back of the restaurant. I'll let Holly know where you've gone. And if you want lunch, I'll have her deliver it to you there."

Eve shook her head. "I've lost my appetite."

Rather than respond, he followed Eve as she led the way through the now crowded diner. People spoke to her but gave him suspicious looks. He knew those looks. He'd grown up in a small town. The same small town as Eve, just a short distance from Austin.

The "private room" at the back of the restaurant appeared to be an afterthought. It was a small room with three tables joined together and a painted plywood wall separating it from the rest of the café. He pulled a chair away from the table and Eve gave him a look. Thanking him. Or possibly telling him she didn't appreciate his help. He didn't know the protocol for helping someone in a wheelchair.

He didn't know this woman. Six years ago he would have said he knew her better than he knew himself. He had been wrong. The woman who had shared everything with him had been someone else. Maybe they hadn't known each other at all.

The girl from his childhood would have turned to him, not away from him.

"I didn't know you had a child," she said.

He sat down across from her, Tori picking at his ear. He held her tight and tried to find the right words. As angry as he might be, he still had to tell her news that would devastate her. News she should have heard two weeks ago.

"She isn't mine. If you weren't hiding, you'd know that. If you'd let your parents tell me how to contact you, you'd know."

"I'm sorry," she murmured, glancing away as she made the apology.

Anger simmered, with her, with himself for caring.

"I found you because my sister saw your name mentioned in an article about Mercy Ranch. I've known you almost my entire life and I've spent four years not knowing where you were or what had happened to you.

So, yeah, you're sorry, but I'm afraid sorry doesn't fix this."

"This?" Her expression was calm. Her dark eyes had settled on Tori, revealing she was anything but calm. A storm brewed in those eyes.

"Tori is James and Hanna's daughter."

She sat perfectly still but her expression clouded at the mention of their friends. He thought she held her breath, waiting.

He had to say the words. He knew it would devastate her. But from her changing expression, she knew what was coming. "They were killed in a car accident."

She shook her head. "No."

He didn't respond. There was nothing he could say that would make this any easier, so he gave her a few minutes to process. In the past he would have held her, comforted her. Now he sat there with his arms around Tori and he wished he knew what to do.

"I…" Her words broke off on a sob. He pulled napkins from the metal holder in the center of the table. She took them and wiped at the steady stream of tears trickling down her cheeks.

In his arms, Tori shifted to look at her, watching intently. Her big blue eyes watered and her lips puckered.

"And Tori?" she asked after a moment.

"Yours and mine." He said it softly, then waited, watching as the news sank in.

Eve rolled back a bit from the table, shaking her head. "What does that mean?"

"It means I got a call from an attorney, informing me that James and Hanna had a will, probably written up before…" He let the sentence trail off. They both knew what *before* meant. "They must not have had it changed because they asked us to raise any child, male or female born to them, should something make it impossible for them to raise that child."

"That can't be. They wouldn't have done that, considering the circumstances."

"I'm sure if they'd thought something like this would happen, they would have changed their will. But the will was written when they thought we would get married. They thought you would come to your senses and…" He sighed.

"They would want her with a couple, with two people, a family." The words ended on a sob. "I'm so sorry. I didn't know. I had no way."

"No, you didn't have a way of knowing." He left it at that.

"What were they thinking?" she repeated.

"It doesn't matter what they were thinking, this is the way it is. James was a planner and they made us the guardians of their child. I am assuming he thought you would surface and things would work out. He only failed to plan one thing, an alternate plan. And there's no one else. Hanna was raised by grandparents who are now too feeble to care for an infant. And James had only his father and he's still in the military. Single and stationed in Italy. He wants to know his granddaughter but he obviously can't raise her."

Eve's eyes closed. When she opened them, he had to turn away from her grief, her pain. He couldn't deal with that, not at the moment.

At the moment he was busy reminding himself of

how she'd hurt him. He reminded himself that she'd cut him out of her life.

The door to the meeting room opened. The waitress, or perhaps owner of the establishment, entered. Her concerned gaze focused in on Eve, on her tears. She shot him a look that told him he was to blame. And boy, was she was going to blame him.

She set the tray she carried on the table and gave Eve a quick hug.

"Eve, honey, is there anything I can get you?"

Eve smiled up at the other woman. "I'm good, Holly, but thank you."

"Okay, but if there's anything I can do." She picked up a bowl of mashed potatoes. "I brought this for the little one. And a bowl of green beans."

"Thank you," Ethan told her.

She gave him a frosty look but she put a plate in front of him, another in front of Eve. "Kylie ordered for the two of you."

"Thank her for me." Eve smiled up at the woman.

"You got it." And then she was gone, the door shutting firmly behind her.

"You seem to have settled here," Ethan observed. He picked up a spoon and gave the child in his arms a small bite after making sure it was cool.

"I have. Ethan, I'm sorry."

"Sorry?" He watched as Tori reached for a green bean.

"Yes, I'm sorry I hurt you. I'm sorry about James and Hanna. I'm so sorry."

"You should have trusted me enough to at least tell

me. You should have included me in the decision to end our relationship."

"You would have tried to convince me that we would be fine. That you would have taken on anything, even though it wasn't what you'd signed on for. And then you would have resented me. Or I would have felt guilty. Either way it was a recipe for disaster."

"I guess I can understand how you would have allowed yourself to believe that. But it wasn't fair, not to me or to friends who loved and missed you and didn't understand why you walked out of our lives."

"I hope someday you can forgive me."

"I hope so, too, because it appears we are tied to one another for the next eighteen years."

"Eighteen years?" She shook her head, not getting his meaning.

"We're raising a child together, Eve. We are her legal guardians, you and I. The state of Texas would like for us to have a plan for her future. James and Hanna were counting on us providing a home for her."

"How are we supposed to do that? As you can see, I'm not exactly in a position to be a parent. We aren't married. So exactly how is this supposed to work?"

"Why aren't you in a position to be a parent?"

She gave him a puzzled look and then pointed down. "Hello? Surely you have eyes."

He did have eyes. And he wished he wasn't seeing the woman he'd planned to marry. He wished his heart wasn't seeing her in a way that almost hurt. The pain was too much. He preferred anger. Anger reminded him how it had felt to receive a Dear John phone call from her.

"I have eyes. I see a woman who is obviously very capable."

"Yes, capable of caring for herself. There's the other little issue you haven't thought about. I live in Oklahoma, not Texas."

"That's definitely an issue but one we can work out. I don't have a lot of time to discuss this. I have a meeting in Tulsa. Forester Farm Sales is opening a new dealership up here."

"I can make this quick and easy. I think the best way to work this out is for me to give you full custody of Tori." Something about the look in her eyes shifted his opinions, made him reconsider his plan of action.

"The truth is, I don't have a clue what I'm doing. It's been two weeks, and in that time we've been working through paperwork, coming to terms with what has happened and just getting by. My mom helps when she can but she's busy running the ranch alongside my dad. My sister, Bethany, has helped from time to time but she's in her last year of nursing school."

"Ethan, I can't do this."

He pushed aside compassion and stood. "I need to run out to the car. Can you hold her?"

She sighed but gave a slight nod. Knowing her the way he did, he recognized the look of longing as she focused on the baby in his arms.

"I can hold her."

He pushed the bowl of mashed potatoes across the table, then he circled around to her side and placed the groggy little girl in her arms. Tori immediately nestled in. It had been a long day. And Eve's arms went around her, holding her close.

It was a dirty move on his part. He hadn't really planned it but he didn't know what else to do. Eve had been his friend for longer than she'd been the woman he loved. He had thought to find a stranger. Instead he found the girl he used to know. And he could see that she'd lost more than the use of her legs. She'd lost her way.

He didn't want to care but he had to. For her sake. For Tori's. So as he walked away from the diner, he told himself he didn't feel guilty for what he was about to do. He would come back. He wasn't the one who disappeared without a word to the people in his life.

But today, Eve deserved a lesson.

Chapter Two

"He isn't coming back." Eve looked from the child in her arms to the friend sitting across from her, a bemused, or maybe amused, look on her face.

"Of course he's coming back." Kylie repeated the same answer she'd been giving for the past fifteen minutes, since Ethan had run out to the car.

Eve shook her head, unwilling to be placated. Fear had been growing inside her, or perhaps panic. Ethan had brought a child, dumped said child in her lap and left. One of two things could be happening. Either he wanted to teach her a lesson or he wanted out of the responsibility that had been handed to them.

They were guardians of the little girl she held in her arms. It wasn't possible. They were the last two people who should be pushed together to care for a child.

"He can't leave me to take care of this child alone." She pushed her wheelchair back a foot, trying to see out the window. Tori squirmed and nearly slid off her lap.

Kylie reached to steady the child's precarious position.

"See, this is why I don't and won't have children. I can't even keep her safely on my lap."

"There are ways." Kylie, always the optimist.

"Of course there are ways," Eve muttered. She didn't even know what car to look for. "He isn't coming back."

"Try the number that called earlier."

"Oh, good idea. There's no caller ID but I should be able to call."

"Is everything okay in here?" Holly asked as she brushed a strand of dark hair back from her face. She took a seat across from Eve.

"Oh, just wonderful." Eve listened to the voice message of Ethan Forester. "Please leave a message," it prompted. So she did. "This isn't fair. You can't do this to Tori. Call me and please tell me you're coming back."

"He got in a Ford truck and scooted on down the street," Holly said after the call ended. "I'm sorry. I would have stopped him if I'd known he was pulling a fast one on you."

"Not a fast one, just…" Eve sighed as she glanced down at the sleeping child. Six months old, the child didn't know much about her life. But she had to know an emptiness where her parents had been. She had to know that everything was topsy-turvy right now.

"She's beautiful," Holly cooed, leaning to brush a finger down Tori's cheek.

"She is," Kylie agreed. She held Cara, her foster daughter, in her arms.

Eve glanced up at Holly. "You have dark rings under your eyes. You're obviously not getting enough sleep. Your mom?"

"Off her meds again. It's a battle."

"I'm sorry," Kylie spoke softly from across the table. "Can we do anything to help?"

"No, there's nothing. It's been my life for, well, my whole life. You would think I'd be used to it."

"But you know how life can be when it's good. I'm sure that makes the turmoil all the more obvious." Kylie reached for Holly's hand and gave it a squeeze.

Holly nodded but her attention shifted back to the baby Eve held. "I'm not here to talk about me. It's obvious Eve has her own drama today. And I'm more than a little curious. So if you really want to take pity on me..."

Eve managed to laugh. "Ex-fiancé."

Holly's eyes widened. "Wowza. And you broke it off with him?"

Eve nodded.

"I'm not sure if we can continue to be friends." Holly laughed as she said it. "He's tall, dark, beyond handsome, knows how to hold a baby. And you dumped him?"

"She obviously martyred herself," Kylie offered.

"Not helping." Eve shot her friend a look.

"Truth hurts," Kylie shot back.

"The baby is his?" Holly asked.

"No." Eve glanced down at the sleeping baby girl. "She's the daughter of our best friends, James and Hanna. They were killed. I guess in an accident. I can't remember if he told me."

The grief washed over her again, squeezing her heart until she wanted to beg for mercy. She'd been so selfish. She'd been so focused on her own life. She hadn't even known. She had no one to blame but herself.

"I can't believe they're gone." Her arms went a little tighter around the sleeping child.

"Wow, that's tough." Holly bent to kiss the top of Eve's head. "I'm sorry, I have to get back to work. Let me know if I can get you anything."

Thirty minutes had passed since Ethan's rapid departure. The clock on the wall continued to tick away the seconds, the minutes. She looked at Kylie.

"He'll be back," Kylie assured her. "Maybe he needed to hit the gas station. Or rent a hotel room."

"He isn't coming back. He would have answered the phone."

"We can't stay here all day," Kylie said. Cara had fallen asleep in her arms. "We should head back to the ranch."

"To do what? I don't know the first thing about taking care of a baby."

"Start by calling her Tori. That's her name. And she's precious. Look at her, Eve. Say something to her."

"You have beautiful eyes," Eve cooed to the little girl. Tori, all blond curls, blue eyes and dimples, grinned. She looked like Hanna. Eve felt a sob rising up in her throat, but she refused to give it room to escape. Her throat tightened with the effort. She closed her eyes and shook her head against the onslaught of emotions.

"I can't do this."

"You can," Kylie insisted. "You're strong. You're capable."

"Right, I can take care of myself. But I can't take care of a child. Not on a daily basis. Watching yours for a few hours is easy. They walk, talk and can go potty all by themselves. Cara being the exception. This—" she held the baby away from her "—this is toxic."

"She needs her diaper changed."

Eve shuddered. "Why isn't she potty trained?"

"Because she's six months old. Don't worry, you can do this. And he'll be back. He's only been gone for a half an hour."

"You don't know him the way I know him."

"Yeah, about that." Kylie grew serious and Eve knew more questions were coming. "Why didn't I know about Mr. Tall, Dark and Handsome?"

"Because you didn't need to know. I ended it and we both moved on."

"I don't think moving on is as easy as saying the words," Kylie said as she grabbed a diaper and wipes from the bag Ethan had left behind. A bag with several outfits, more than enough diapers, bottles, food and formula.

"It was for the best," Eve defended. "It was the right thing to do."

Kylie shook her head. "Right thing for who? You or him?"

"That isn't fair."

"Isn't it?" Kylie asked. "You decided for him that he didn't want to be married to someone in a wheelchair."

"Someone he would have to take care of for the rest of his life."

Kylie arched a brow at that. "Really? Because who is taking care of you now?"

Eve ignored the question. Kylie shook her head.

"Give me that baby. I'll change her diaper." Kylie settled Cara in her car seat and reached for Tori. "But you'll have to change the next diaper."

"You say that as if I'm going to have her for a while. I'm clearly not cut out for this. I was an only child, raised by parents who had me late in life. We didn't socialize with people who had small children. I didn't babysit for neighbors. I'm very unqualified for this. Why would Hanna and James think that I could be the person this baby girl needs?"

"They obviously knew you better than you know yourself. They believed you could do this. I believe you can do this."

"That's great, I'm glad everyone believes in me. But Tori deserves more. She deserves love and security." Eve shook her head at the great expanse of sadness opening up inside her. "Ethan has to come back. He can't abandon her this way."

"I doubt he plans to abandon her. Now I'm going to change Tori and then we'll get you both back to the ranch and settled in your place."

"Alone?" Eve hoped she'd misunderstood. She considered herself a strong, independent woman. But a baby, by herself? All night?

Kylie gave her a quick hug. "Don't look so lost. I promise you'll get through this."

"I hope you're right, about him coming back and about surviving this." She looked at the baby Kylie now held. "I hope she survives me."

Kylie laughed at that. "You'll both survive. Eve, you're more than able."

Would it do any good to admit she was scared to death? Probably not. Admitting fear wasn't what she did. Ever. "Of course I am."

An hour later Eve wasn't convinced she would survive, not even for an afternoon.

She held Tori on her lap as Kylie showed her how to

use the baby sling she'd picked up at her house. Kylie slid the cloth behind Eve's back, settled Tori on her lap and then wrapped the baby with the cloth so that the sling held her securely in Eve's lap.

"This will enable you to hold her and still maneuver." Kylie made sure the cloth was secure. "It's soft so you can keep it behind your back and when you pick her up, just wrap it around her and secure it."

"Okay, that's one hurdle. There are just so many things I've never considered, never thought I would have to consider." Eve brushed her cheek against the top of Tori's head. "I didn't think she'd smell like baby powder and happiness. Ugh, listen to me. I don't talk this way."

Kylie sat on the sofa facing her as Tori snuggled in close, eventually becoming a heavy, sleepy weight against Eve's shoulder.

"She's very happy cuddled up to you."

Eve kissed the little head that was tucked against her. "Yes, she's happy for now. But later she'll want bottles. She'll be hungry. And where will she sleep?"

"She'll have to sleep with you. We'll push your bed against the wall and you can put her on the inside. You can take a bottle with you, in case she wakes up during the night."

"Changing diapers?" Eve tossed out the next hurdle.

"There's a changing pad in the diaper bag. You can put it on your desk. That gives you the ability to roll close and change her without having to bend over the sofa or bed," Kylie offered, not seeing obstacles but solutions. That was her natural personality. Kylie was a problem solver.

The front door opened and Eve hoped beyond hope

that it would be Ethan. Instead it was Sierra. She, Kylie and Eve had once been roommates. They'd had other roommates along the way but the three of them had been fixtures at the ranch since almost the beginning. Now it was just Sierra and Eve. They shared the main living area of the one-time garage turned apartment building but they each had their own bedroom, bathroom and sitting area.

Sierra looked from Kylie to Eve to the baby and froze, her eyes going wide. "No."

She walked on to the kitchen with just that word but as she poured a cup of coffee, she shook her head. "Nope."

"You don't have a choice and neither does Eve. For the time being you have a new roommate." Kylie shot Sierra a warning look. "And you'll love her."

"I don't think so. Babies smell, they cry, they need constant attention. Why is she here? Is there something you haven't told us, Eve?" Sierra wandered into the living room with her coffee. She stared down at the baby on Eve's lap and shook her head again. "It's cute, but I guarantee you, it won't be cute for long. They're like puppies. They grow up."

"You're horrible," Kylie said. "And the baby is a *she*, not an *it*."

"I'm horrible but I'm honest about babies." Sierra grinned at their ex-roommate, her expression softening. "I'm the person who never pets the cute puppies you all raise. I don't go all dewy eyed over a new foal. I told you the truth when Cara was born. Everyone else lied. She wasn't the prettiest baby ever. I mean, she's pretty now, but that first day, not so cute. She was red, wrinkled and cried a lot."

"But you'll help Eve if she needs it?" Kylie prodded.

Sierra sat down next to Kylie and eventually she nodded. "Because we're friends, I'll help you out, Eve. But where in the world did this little bundle of joy come from?"

"From my past," Eve said. She avoided eye contact with her friends because any hint of sympathy would bring tears.

"She showed up on our doorstep? Or did you find her under a cabbage leaf? You're killing me here." Sierra stretched her legs, grimacing just a bit at the movement.

"She's the daughter of friends," Eve started and then she told the rest of the story, managing to hold it together. As she spoke, she found herself holding Tori a little closer.

"Wow," Sierra said quietly. "That's a lot, Eve. I am sorry."

"Me, too."

"You had a fiancé," Sierra said after a moment.

"Yes, I had a fiancé."

"And you've misplaced him again?" Sierra teased.

"I didn't misplace him. I gave him an out. And this time, he took the out."

"This is way more reality than I like to deal with on a Monday afternoon," Sierra said as she stood, grabbing her coffee cup off the end table. "I'll help when I can but Jack has me busy with this lovely wedding chapel idea of his."

Eve laughed at that. "You're such a romantic, you'll make a great wedding planner."

"Yeah, well, right now, being a wedding planner is far more appealing than changing dirty diapers. You have fun with that and I'll see you all later."

Eve pressed her lips to Tori's head, amazed that in a few short hours she'd found it so easy to love one small child.

Until Ethan returned, Eve would manage to care for Tori. She would give the little girl all the love and hugs she could, not that it would make up for the loss of her parents. But Ethan would return, he had to. When he did, Eve would explain that she just couldn't be a part of parenting Tori full-time.

Tuesday morning Ethan followed his GPS to Mercy Ranch, just a few miles outside Hope and a ninety-minute drive from Tulsa. He pulled up to the main house, a two-story log home with plenty of windows, big covered porches and a yellow Labrador sprawled out in a flower bed. A man walked down off the back porch, pulling his hat low as he headed in Ethan's direction.

Ethan got out of his truck, grabbing his hat from the backseat as he did. When he turned around, the other man stood just feet away. He was close to Ethan in age with a jagged scar on the left side of his face and steel-gray eyes that could nail a man to the wall.

"Good morning," Ethan greeted.

"I'm guessing you're the missing fiancé? Or should I say, AWOL fiancé?" The man spoke without a lot of warmth in his voice.

"Ex-fiancé, and I'm not the one who went missing. I knew where I was the whole time." Ethan kept his tone casual. No reason to make enemies here.

"You're brave, I'll give you that," the man said as he tipped his hat back a bit. A slow grin slid across his face. "Name's Isaac West."

Ethan held out a hand. "Name's Mud. But you can call me Ethan. Ethan Forester."

Isaac West chuckled. "You got the first part right. She's madder than a wet hornet right now."

"But she survived."

"Yeah, she did. But not if you ask her. My fiancée, Rebecca, went down to check on her a bit ago. From what I've been told, there was more formula on her and the counter than in the baby. And she might have been wearing bananas on her shirt."

"Maybe I should rethink going down there?"

"I think if you try to leave, she will hunt you down and hurt you. But I can walk you down there, if you'd like. Safety in numbers and all that."

Ethan wouldn't call himself weak. He'd been on some pretty rank horses, ridden bulls, and he'd even back-talked his mama. That last one had proved to be more stupid than brave.

"If you want to show me where to find her," he said in accepting the offer, "I wouldn't be opposed."

Isaac pounded him on the back in good-natured camaraderie. "You got it."

The ranch was a sprawling place, clean with good fences, cattle and horses grazing in the fields, a nice stable and several residences. In the corral near the stable he could see men working with horses. A short distance away, it appeared a new stable was being built.

Isaac followed his interested gaze and chuckled. "Wedding venue. It's going to look like a stable. The main area will be the chapel, the indoor 'arena' will be for receptions. My dad guesses it'll keep a few of the residents busy with managing, cleaning and catering."

"This is quite a setup. I'm impressed."

Isaac shrugged at the compliment. "It was all Jack. He's the idea man. He keeps everyone busy and moving, even if he's slowing down a little. Parkinson's."

"I'm sorry."

"Don't tell him that. He's still in charge and his housekeeper doesn't let grass grow under his feet."

"I read an article that he also bought an older resort and remodeled, as well as a bait shop."

"Yep, he's managed to put about two dozen veterans to work. We usually have ten to twelve people living on the ranch at any given time. After a while they usually head back to where they came from. A few stay and find a place to call home in Hope."

"And you?" Ethan asked, taking a guess that he was a veteran as well as Jack's son.

"Guess I'm not going anywhere since I grew up here. And if you're asking if I'm a veteran, I am."

They were approaching a metal building that appeared to have been a garage at one time. The multiple windows, covered patio and French doors indicated it had been remodeled to house veterans. From inside he heard a baby crying. Isaac glanced at him, grinning.

"That doesn't sound good." Ethan slowed his steps, needing a minute to collect himself before he faced Eve. He hadn't felt the best when he woke up that morning, attributing it to something he'd eaten the day before. Now he definitely felt his stomach tighten and he decided it was a case of nerves.

"Cold feet?" Isaac asked as he knocked on the door. "Are you regretting leaving her with the baby?"

"Nope."

The door opened. A woman, tall with long auburn hair and a weary look in her hazel eyes, greeted them. The expression shifted to angry when she saw him standing behind Isaac.

"Having a bad day, Sierra?" Isaac pulled off his hat, grinning as if he didn't see the storm coming.

"Oh, I'm having a lovely day. After a sleepless night." She waved them inside, her expression going from angry to glacial when she looked at Ethan. "I'm assuming you're the one who abandoned that poor baby girl."

"I didn't abandon her," he defended. But he wouldn't say more, not to this woman.

The other woman in the room, he guessed he would have to say something to her. She held Tori in her arms as tears streamed down the baby girl's face. Eve looked exhausted and close to tears. He hadn't expected it to be quite this traumatic. For either of them.

"How dare you," she spat.

He stepped forward and held his arms out to Tori. She reached for him, sobbing.

"You can't explain to a six-month-old that the person they need is coming back. Or that the person they need is being selfish, rotten, horrible…"

"Shh," he whispered to Tori, holding her close. He rocked back and forth, whispering comforting words. His mom had taught him this trick. It also worked to calm Eve. She quieted, still glaring but no longer spewing harsh words at him.

That was good, because he needed a minute to breathe.

"I guess I shouldn't ask how it went?" he spoke softly.

"She didn't sleep. And I didn't know what to do to help her." Eve's voice trailed off on a sigh. "You could have asked. You could have told me what to do for her, what she likes. Instead you just walked out."

"Shh," he tried again, hoping that it would again work on Eve. He stood in the middle of the oversize living room with early morning sunlight streaming through kitchen windows and Tori cuddled against his shoulder. Eve sat a few feet away from him looking ready to spit nails.

"I didn't plan on leaving," he told her in a whisper. "I had to make a call. I got to the car and it hit me that you would never agree to this guardianship. I knew you would come up with dozens of reasons why you can't."

"And I would have been right."

He glanced down at the child sleeping in his arms. He'd had a couple of weeks to get used to the idea of parenting her, of being a dad. He'd come to terms with the big changes in his life because she was in it. Like Eve, he'd had a lot of reasons why he couldn't.

Those reasons still crept up on him from time to time. Usually in the middle of the night when he couldn't sleep, or Tori couldn't sleep. He'd hired a nanny. That didn't really suffice. Mrs. Porter wasn't looking for another child to raise. She showed Tori a lot of love, but she'd made it clear from the beginning she could nanny but she wasn't the parent. He couldn't give that duty over to someone else.

"I'm sorry, Eve, but I had to do something to make you see how important this is. We can't just walk away from her. It might not be what we signed on for and I feel like I'm the last person who should be raising this little girl, but James and Hanna trusted us."

"But there is no *us*," she said with a lift of her chin, but he could see pain reflected in her dark eyes.

The pain he saw didn't bother him as much as what he didn't see in her eyes, in her expression. He didn't see the person he used to know, the woman he'd planned to marry.

He had noticed the same yesterday, and he guessed that's why he'd left Tori with her. He'd been sitting there looking at a woman he used to think he knew better than he knew himself, and he hadn't recognized her.

"There is no *us*, but we still exist, you and me, and Tori needs us." He said it softly because the little girl in his arms seemed to be drifting off, even with the occasional sob.

"There has to be another option. I obviously can't do this. Last night was proof."

"Last night meant nothing. You've always managed, Eve. You're strong and capable."

"Before, Ethan. I was that person before. This is me now, and I can't."

"I guess you have changed. I've never heard you say you can't do anything."

He sat down on a nearby chair. Isaac had left. The woman named Sierra had also disappeared. They were alone. When had they last been alone? The night he proposed? It had been the night she left for Afghanistan. He'd taken her to dinner in San Antonio and they'd walked along the riverfront surrounded by people, music and twinkling lights.

He'd dropped to one knee there in front of strangers passing by, seeing the sights. Dozens had stopped to watch as she cried and said yes. Later they'd made the drive to the airport, his ring glistening on her finger, planning a wedding that would never happen.

"Ethan?" Her voice was soft, quiet, questioning.

He glanced down at the little girl in his arms.

"What other option is there, Eve? Should we turn her over to the state, let her take her chances with whoever they choose? Should we find some distant relative? What do you recommend?"

He leaned back in the chair and studied her face, her expression. She was everything familiar. His childhood friend. The person he'd loved. *Had* loved. Past tense. The woman he'd wanted to spend his life with had been someone else, someone who never backed down. She looked as tough, as stubborn as ever, but there was something fragile in her expression.

Something in her expression made him recheck his feelings. He'd been bucked off horses, trampled by a bull, broken his arm jumping dirt bikes. She'd been his only broken heart. He didn't want another one.

"There is no *us*, you've made that clear." He loosened his hold on Tori and she sighed in her sleep. "I'm glad you thought that was your decision to make and that I had no say in the matter. That is beside the point. There is a Tori. And she needs a home. She needs us. You and me."

"She is obviously bonded to you. You've figured this parenting thing out." Her voice took on a frantic tone.

"No, I haven't figured it out. I have help. My mom. My sister. But they can't raise her." Not that he hadn't considered it. He could go to court, get custody finalized and then give guardianship to his sister, Bethany.

"What are we supposed to do?" Eve asked, moving closer, her gaze landing on the child in his arms.

"That's why I'm here," he admitted. "So we can figure this out. The judge wants this case settled. He's given me temporary guardianship but he wants to be able to finalize her guardianship and he wants it done as soon as possible. He believes James and Hanna made a decision based on the facts they had and that they had a reason for the choice they made. There's a court date in six weeks."

"Court?"

"In Texas. And you have to be there. We both have to go and we need to have a plan in place by then."

"A plan?"

He tried to hide the hint of a smile her questions instigated. "A plan for Tori, for us, for the future."

She shook her head. "My future is here. You have a life in Texas. We can't shift her back and forth like some unwanted little parcel. That wouldn't give her the stability she needs or the family she deserves."

She was right. They weren't a couple. They hadn't been for several years. And, if it had been that easy for her to end things, maybe they had never truly been a couple.

That realization didn't help solve the problem at hand. Tori's dependence on them to make the right choices. Like it or not, they were in this together.

Chapter Three

She couldn't do this. She didn't know what "this" meant. It seemed to be a whole list of things. She couldn't be a parent. She couldn't process the loss of friends she hadn't spoken to in years. The loss was real, even with the passing of time.

Her gaze landed on their little girl. The peaceful, sleeping child in Ethan's arms.

Ethan. She looked up and found him watching her, questions burning in his blue eyes. He was at the top of the list of things she couldn't tackle. Not right now with her emotions shattered.

She pushed her chair away from him and headed for the door, fighting tears, fighting with the past. As she went out the door, she heard him call her name. She shook her head. Not because she wouldn't deal with this situation but because she needed a few minutes alone to figure out the next step.

She needed to pray. Her heart constricted at the thought of prayer. Because she did pray. She went to church. Sometimes she sang in the choir. But when anyone said to trust God, she felt a spike of true anger rise up in her spirit. Because she had trusted Him. She'd prayed. She'd believed.

And here she was. James and Hanna were gone and it wasn't right. She wanted to scream to heaven that it wasn't fair. And where was God in all this?

With no clear destination in mind she found herself at the kennel. She opened a gate and whistled to the dog inside. The yellow Labrador retriever immediately moved to her side, probably glad to escape the kennel and her puppies. The dogs training to be service animals were typically housed with either the men or women on the ranch, so they were socialized and immersed in training.

In the beginning, the dogs had been a hobby and therapy. With time, experience and training, Mercy Ranch had become a key provider of service dogs to members of the military and to other deserving folks around the country.

"How's the family?" Eve asked the dog. In response, April gave her a sloppy dog kiss. "Eight puppies. You're an expert. Do you have any advice for me?"

April sat next to Eve's chair, waiting expectantly.

"I didn't think so." Eve closed her eyes and waited for an answer, for some clear response to the turmoil she felt. Tori was James and Hanna's daughter. She was a tiny little girl without parents. She needed people to count on.

Then there was Ethan. She'd always loved him. From the time they'd been in elementary school and he'd told a bully to stop picking on her, she'd loved him. She'd loved him at sixteen when he'd punched Brandon Parker for saying something rude in the hall at school. She'd loved him more at twenty when he'd sent her a dozen roses and told her she was stuck with him. Forever.

And she'd loved him when she told him they could no longer get married. She'd convinced herself that was the biggest act of love. For four years she'd been telling herself she was over him. That she'd done the right thing and they'd both moved on.

April nudged at her hand and she slid her fingers through the animal's soft fur, pulling her close and leaning to bury her face in the dog's neck. She had to pull it together and find a way to convince Ethan to leave.

"Running?"

She looked up, startled by the question. She hadn't heard anyone approaching. She smiled at Joe Chapman. He'd been at the ranch almost as long as any of them. He had an easy demeanor, always pleasant. She thought he worked hard at that persona. But inside he was as angry as the rest of them. He'd lost an arm and one side of his face was scarred.

She no longer noticed Joe's scars. He was just Joe. And he was waiting for an answer.

"No, not running. I'm just trying to figure out how to tell my past to stay in the past."

"It isn't always that easy."

"You've managed," she said with a smile to soften the words. If he was going to get in her business, she'd get in his.

"Yeah, well, my parents don't want much to do with me. I'm not living up to their expectations."

"It seems our parents are opposite ends of the spectrum. Mine would love for me to come home so they could smother me with love and attention. I think they would only see the chair and I'd cease to exist."

"Yeah, I get that. My parents can't see beyond their career goals for their children."

She felt sorry for baiting him. "Yeah, I know."

"That's why we love Mercy Ranch. Jack gave us a place to be ourselves."

"We're not hiding?" she asked her friend.

He shrugged. "We probably are."

"So you heard about the baby?"

He laughed at the question. "Who hasn't heard about her? And heard her. She's got a powerful set of lungs."

"Yes, yes she does." She raised a finger and the dog sat. When she pointed to the ground, the dog dropped to her belly. "You're still the best, April."

"You trained her. You get some of the credit."

She smiled up at Joe. "Thanks. But let's talk about the elephant in the room. Or the baby. Am I a coward?"

"I don't think so." He'd taken a seat on the nearby bench but he stood, rubbing at his left shoulder. "But I am, so I'm going to head out. Kylie at twelve o'clock."

He saluted and headed for the stable. As Kylie approached, clearing her throat to make herself known, Eve pointed to the kennel. With head down and reluctant steps, April entered the kennel to be attacked by her eight super hungry puppies.

"You need to come back to the house," Kylie said.

"Because I'm avoiding and I can't avoid?"

"No, because Ethan is sick. Sierra had to go back to the house to get something and found him leaning over the trash can. Tori was on a blanket on the floor crying."

Eve looked heavenward. "This is what happens when I ask for help."

Kylie grabbed the handles of Eve's chair and turned her toward the apartment. "At least you're praying about it."

Her struggles with faith weren't exactly secret. Kylie observed things. It wasn't a discussion they'd had but Eve wasn't surprised to know her friend had figured it out.

"Yes, praying, ranting, same thing I guess."

"Sometimes," Kylie agreed. "And I think God is okay with our honest emotions."

Eve certainly hoped so. She didn't feel a need to respond and Kylie didn't push her to keep talking.

"Where are your kids?" Eve asked when they were halfway to the entrance of the building she'd called home for several years. They affectionately called it "the garage."

"With Maria and Jack. They made cookies."

"Cara made cookies? She can't even eat cookies."

"She's watching from her infant swing," Kylie responded. Eve could hear the contentment in her voice, picture the happy smile on her face.

It was true, what the Bible said, that things did work together for good for those who trusted. And if anyone deserved that, it was Kylie. She'd loved Carson West since junior high and somehow the two had found each other again.

"You changed the subject," Kylie said as she pushed the chair onto the sidewalk.

"Did I?" Eve took control of her chair, pushing the wheels quickly to reach the door of the apartment.

Kylie stepped between her and the door. "It isn't always cut-and-dried. You know that. Faith gets tested. We all go through storms."

"Some of us get stranded on a deserted island." The words slipped out, then Eve backed away from the door, from her friend.

Kylie's expression didn't register surprise. Eve didn't know how. She felt surprised by what she'd said, surprised by the emotions that accompanied the words.

"That's pretty powerful," Kylie finally said. "Maybe that's the place where people lose faith or even turn from their faith. Especially if you believe God isn't on that island with you."

"Only a volleyball named Wilson and it doesn't answer. No matter how much you talk to it, shout at it, nothing." Eve closed her eyes. "I'm pathetic."

"Actually, you're not. I just wouldn't have thought to compare God to a volleyball."

Eve gave in to the smile that tugged at her mouth. "Yeah, well, sometimes God is like that volleyball. You keep talking, keeping telling Him what you need and you wonder why He doesn't answer. And then you wonder, does He even hear? Is it all some big joke. So here I sit, thinking my life is the worst, and now this. This isn't really about me, is it? This is about Tori. It's about the loss of two very dear people. But I can't be the person Tori needs me to be."

"You think you can't. But I think of all the other things you said you couldn't do that you've done."

"I still can't walk. Remember those first months when I insisted I would walk again? And I prayed, asking God to show those doctors they were wrong."

God hadn't fixed it. He'd given her the strength to survive it, but not the ability to overcome it.

"Should we start calling those 'volleyball' moments of faith?" Kylie asked, completely serious.

"Yeah, I think so."

"Tom Hanks got off the island. He actually pursued Wilson, went after him. And while pursuing, he was rescued."

"He went back to a life that was completely different and looked nothing like the life he'd known."

"We're never the same, Eve. The things we go through change us. We're like a riverbed, always shifting, always changing."

"You're so smart," Eve told her friend. "Seriously, Kylie, I'm not sure I would have survived without you."

"You would have survived. Your deserted island isn't so deserted. And He's listening, even when you think He isn't."

God. Of course He was. She hadn't abandoned her faith. Sometimes she felt it had abandoned her. From inside the apartment she could hear crying. She had to go in. Had to face Ethan and make a plan.

"Here we go," she said.

Kylie pushed the door open and Eve entered ahead of her. Ethan was in the bathroom, and Sierra sat on the sofa holding Tori away from her. Tori was crying. Sierra wasn't far from it.

Eve bit down on her bottom lip to fight the laughter that bubbled up.

"Don't you dare laugh," Sierra warned. "Seriously, don't."

"You're definitely not on the island alone," Kylie chuckled.

No, Eve wasn't alone. But she did feel a little like she'd stepped back into the world and realized that, once again, everything had changed.

Sprawled out on the sofa, Ethan looked up at the woman looming over him. Okay, she wasn't looming. Peering with disgust, her nose wrinkled, her eyes reflecting…humor?

"It isn't funny." He ground the words out and closed his eyes as another wave of nausea hit.

"You have to get him out of here," the roommate with the auburn hair spoke from behind Eve. "Seriously, he's contaminating the entire place. We'll all be sick."

"What do you expect me to do with him?" Eve shot back. She turned her chair a bit.

He opened his eyes and saw that her friend had picked up Tori and was settling her in Eve's lap. Maybe he hadn't planned to get sick but he couldn't help seeing the benefits. Eve holding Tori close while she surveyed what had to be his less than pleasing appearance.

The roommate gave a disgusted groan.

"Drag him out by his feet. I don't care what you do with him. Just get him out."

"Calm down," Kylie ordered. "We'll take him to Jack's. If we confine him to the upstairs, no one else will catch it."

"I'm sure we're already exposed," Eve reasoned.

"Bleach," Sierra said. "Spray him down with bleach. Spray the couch with bleach."

Eve started to laugh. The sound took him by surprise, even if he didn't appreciate it at that particular moment.

"Who knew you were a germaphobe?" she told her friend.

"I'm not. I just enjoy good health and want to keep it that way. Could you please, please get him out of here?" She shoved the trash can at him and walked away.

Moments later he could hear water running in the kitchen.

"We need a plan," Eve said.

"Right now?" Ethan asked. "I'm sure this is only a twenty-four-hour thing. I just need to find a place to let it run its course."

"Tori?" she spoke softly.

"You can do this, Eve."

"What if she gets sick, too?"

"She's always been healthy," he assured her. "I'm always healthy."

"Yeah, until now. Should I call someone? Your mom? She could come up and take care of you."

"I'm thirty-one years old, not three. I can take care of myself. And if you meant to ask my mom to come up and take care of Tori, no. Just no. She's busy with the ranch and with the guesthouse."

"I know."

He shot her a look. "Call *your* mom and ask for help."

"No fair."

"Maybe not, but I don't think you realize how much you've hurt them by pushing them out of your life."

She opened her mouth and he knew she meant to deny the accusation but then she didn't. Instead she glanced away but not before he saw a flicker of pain in her eyes.

"I'm sorry," he said.

"You're not the one who has to apologize."

He would have said more but another wave of nausea hit. She backed away from him, clearly trying to distance herself from whatever virus had him in its grip.

"Do you think you can make it to Jack's?" Kylie West asked after a few minutes. "I called Isaac and he's unlocking the back door. You can go upstairs and we'll quarantine you in a room with a bathroom."

"I can make it," he said. "I could even rent a room if there's one available. I don't want to make anyone else sick."

"I'm sure it's too late for that!" the redheaded roommate yelled from some distant part of the house.

Eve laughed. "This is almost worth it if it means getting under Sierra's skin."

"Yeah, I did this just for your pleasure." Ethan sat up. Tori grinned at him, that perfect toothless smile of hers that made him realize she was worth the trouble. This might not have been his plan, raising a child, finding Eve, but Tori was worth it. She deserved everything he could give her.

He made eye contact with his former fiancée. Tori deserved Eve. She deserved her love. She deserved her presence in her life.

"There are things you need to know." He got the words out, past a wave of nausea. "Man, this is terrible. I haven't had a virus like this in years. It makes me feel like I'm in grade school all over again."

"If it makes you feel better, you don't look like you're

in grade school. You have a little gray." Eve touched her hair above her ear.

"Yeah, well, I'm a little older than I was the last time I saw you."

Her smile dissolved. "What do I need to know about Tori? Although it might have been helpful if you'd given me this advice yesterday. When you took off and left her with me."

He reached for the bottle of water the unsympathetic roommate had left on the table before she escaped. He presumed it was meant for him. She'd also left crackers.

"So?"

"There are diapers, wipes and food in my car. And a can of formula. I usually keep a bottle of water at night. It's to help wean her from nightly feedings. Or so my mom told me."

"This is temporary, Ethan. I'll help you until you can get back on your feet. But then you have to leave. I can't do this. I..." She looked down at the little girl sitting securely on her lap. Her heart was breaking. He could see it in her expression, as if she was shattered on the inside and no longer believed in her own abilities. But looking around, everything he'd seen, she was accomplished. She had survived and rebuilt her life.

Or so it appeared. Appearances could be deceiving, he knew. His little sister had suffered throughout high school, bullied and beat down by others because of a birthmark on her face. They hadn't known until it was almost too late.

Eve's words made him consider letting her off the hook. He could walk away, pretend she didn't matter to him or to Tori. That would make things easier. He could go to court and tell the judge that he would be the sole provider for Tori and hope for the best.

Nowhere in his plans had he ever seen himself in this role, as a single parent. For that reason, Eve didn't get a pass. She didn't get to wash her hands of this and pretend it didn't affect her.

"You can do this," he assured her.

She didn't look convinced. She looked frightened. And that wasn't the Eve he'd always known. His Evie had been fearless. She'd been the kind of person who took on anyone and anything. Man, he'd missed her. He'd missed her presence more than he could possibly say.

He wondered if any of that Eve remained or if she'd completely abandoned the person he'd known. One thing was for certain, she'd been able to throw away not only a friendship but an engagement. She'd done so without giving him the opportunity to play a part in the decision-making process. That was hard to forgive.

But he would forgive her. In time. They both needed time.

Right now what he needed most was a quiet room and a bed.

Chapter Four

Eve woke up feeling less than rested. Night two with Tori had proved even more restless than the previous evening. She turned her head to the baby lying next to her who slept soundly now, after a night of waking every thirty minutes or so. She was sprawled out, her rosebud mouth open, her baby hands close to her face. That image did something to Eve's heart. Actually, it did everything to her heart. A heart that had been on standby for four years, waiting for her to figure out this new life.

She reached to touch the sleeping baby but pulled back, unwilling to wake her just yet.

Panic set in, telling her Ethan had to leave Hope, take Tori and their past with him. She couldn't do this again, this pain, the letting go. He would have to see that they couldn't raise a child together. He deserved someone who could give him the dreams they'd once shared but could no longer. The ranch, training horses, managing the family business. Tori deserved two parents.

The baby stirred, fussing a little in her sleep. After

a few minutes her eyes opened. She saw Eve and, of course, she cried. Eve wasn't the person she wanted. Big tears rolled down her cheeks and her bottom lip quivered as her eyes drifted around the room. Eve's heart broke all over again.

"You want your mommy, don't you, sweetness?" Eve pulled the baby close to her side. She looked up at the ceiling. "It isn't fair. This isn't the way life should be."

There was no response from Tori. Of course there wasn't. She let out a sigh and refused the thought that tried to puncture her conscience. *Maybe this was the way it was meant to be.*

She shook her head, shook away that thought.

No! Tori should be safely tucked away in a crib somewhere in Texas with Hanna waking up to feed her, change her diaper. James with his messy hair and permanent grin should be hugging them both tight.

This wasn't the plan. This life with Eve fighting against her useless legs, ignoring calls from her parents, smiling and pretending everything was okay in her world. She shook her head to block those self-pitying thoughts. Her life was good. She had friends. She had a community. She had so much to be thankful for.

She sat up, because she wouldn't waste her day feeling sorry for herself. Every now and then the urge to fall into a pity party would sneak up on her, try to keep her in bed. She fought it. The way she'd fought to regain her life.

With practiced ease, she moved her legs to the edge of the bed. Before taking the next step, she drew Tori closer so it would be easier to pull her off the bed and onto her lap. With her legs over the side of the bed, she made the transfer to her wheelchair, got herself settled and then lifted Tori onto her lap. She'd left the baby sling on the dresser, and as she reached for it she realized she had an unexpected problem.

She lifted the baby and wasn't surprised to see the dampness had leaked through to her own cotton pants.

Tori grinned.

"You think that's funny, do you?"

She flashed another toothless grin. Eve fought the connection she felt toward this tiny human being with her soft curls, slobbery grins and smelly diapers.

A light rap on her bedroom door drew her attention away from Miss Stinky Pants. "Yeah?"

"It's Kylie."

"Just in the nick of time. Come in, I'm up."

The door opened and Kylie stepped in, her gaze sliding over Eve to focus on Tori. Eve immediately felt guilty because as much as she didn't want to be the person responsible for the little girl in her arms, Kylie did want the responsibility of babies. Afghanistan had taken Eve's ability to walk and Kylie's ability to have babies of her own.

Kylie would be the last to lament her situation. Especially now. She had Andy and Maggie, Carson's children from his previous marriage. They'd even finalized adoption so that she was legally their mommy.

They were also licensed foster parents, agreeing to love the children God placed in their home. Love them and be willing to let them go. That part would always be painful.

"Why are you holding her like that?" Kylie rushed forward and took the baby.

Her nose wrinkled as she took Tori into her arms.

"I guess no explanation required?" Eve grinned up at her friend.

"None whatsoever. I'll carry her to the living room but you're changing this." Kylie walked out of the room.

"I need to change," Eve called after her friend.

"Quickly!" Kylie yelled back.

"Yeah, because it's easy," Eve grumbled as she headed for the closet.

She found a comfy pair of loose cotton pants. In five minutes she had dry clothes again. She hoped that wouldn't be something she had to do often.

No, of course it wouldn't happen often. Ethan would leave and take Tori with him. As soon as he was healthy and able, he had to go.

"Do you know how Ethan is feeling?" Eve called out as she pulled on the gloves that served several purposes—they kept her hands clean because wheels were dirty, and they kept her hands from becoming sore, blistered and overly calloused.

After pulling her hair into a ponytail, she headed down the wide hallway to the living room. She could smell coffee and something sweet. It had to be sweet. Maybe Sierra had muffins in the oven. She was blessed with a roommate who enjoyed cooking. If not for Sierra and the occasional meal at the main house, Eve would mostly survive on PB&J sandwiches.

"Maria took him coffee and toast, and he seemed better but staying in his room." Kylie smiled. "Carson said he needs to stay away from everyone for at least another twenty-four hours."

"Twenty-four hours is a long time." Eve took Tori

from her friend. She settled the baby on the mat she'd placed on her desk and managed a somewhat sloppy change of diaper.

"You're getting to be an expert."

"A half dozen diapers does not make me an expert." She didn't want to be the expert at changing diapers, nighttime feedings or cuddling with Tori. She didn't want to get attached, only to have Ethan realize she'd been right to end their engagement. "Speaking of, where is Cara?"

"With her mom."

Eve moved Tori from the desk to her lap. The activity gave Kylie a moment to get her emotions under control.

"How's her mother doing?" Eve asked as she wrapped the sling around Tori.

Kylie headed for the kitchen, her back stiff. But Eve heard a sniffle. She followed her friend, stopping once to adjust the baby in her pouch. It caused some maneuverability issues, having an almost twenty-pound baby on her lap.

"She's good, actually. And don't worry, I'm good. The goal is reunification. I knew that going in, and I had the plan that I would give this baby the love she needs while her mommy works through her issues. Glory is a sweet kid. She's only eighteen and she's had a rough life but she wants to do better."

"She should start by not doing drugs while…"

Kylie raised her hand. "Don't. That isn't fair. You don't know her story."

Eve dropped a kiss on Tori's head tucked neatly beneath her chin. "I know and I'm sorry."

"I want Cara to have her mom. If it means helping

Glory get her life together, then that's what Carson and I are prepared to do."

"Uh-oh. What are the two of you plotting?"

"Jack is giving her a job on the ranch, helping with the wedding chapel."

Eve laughed. "Sierra is going to love you."

"Right?" Kylie grinned, her mood lifting. "And Cara will be able to see her mom. It isn't that Glory is a bad person. She just doesn't know a better way."

"She's lucky to have the two of you," Eve said.

"It isn't luck, it's God. He's given us so much and if we can help Cara and Glory have a better life, that's what we have to do."

"I love you, Kylie West. I don't know what I'd do without your friendship and your faith to keep me moving forward. Today especially."

"Is it hard, having him here?" Kylie asked as she set a cup of coffee on a nearby table. "I mean, I know it is. This whole situation is difficult and I'm sorry."

"It's…" She looked down at the smiling baby with her clean diaper. "It's unexpected. And it's painful."

"You know, if you opened up…" Kylie's gentle, therapist voice trailed off.

"Don't. I know all about the lines of communication, and I realize now that I've really messed up. I should have taken your advice. I don't know if I was trying to protect them or myself, but it's pretty obvious I've done a decent job of hurting the people I care about."

"It can be fixed."

She shook her head at that. "No, it can't. Not really. It can be mended but not fixed. I just have to figure out where to start."

"It won't be easy but you have to know, you're in a better place now than you were four years ago."

"You're right. Emotionally I am in a better place. Even physically. I'm stronger, more sure of myself."

Kylie put a plate of muffins on the table. "I hope Sierra didn't mean these for someone special. They're delicious."

"What about the baby?" Eve pulled off her gloves and shoved them in the pouch on the back of her chair. "I'm assuming she has to be fed?"

"You assumed correctly."

Kylie didn't give her a break. She grabbed the handles of the chair and pushed Eve away from the table just as she made a move for a muffin.

"What are you doing?" Eve glanced back at the sugar topped muffins.

"Baby eats first, Mommy."

"I'm not her mommy. Her mommy was Hanna."

Kylie's hand rested on Eve's shoulder. "I know. I'm sorry.

"This stinks."

"I know it does."

"I wish there were easy answers." Eve glanced back at her friend. "You know how I like to jump into things and make spur-of-the-moment decisions."

"Like ending an engagement?"

"Today is about Tori. I can't make a spur-of-the-moment decision regarding this baby. She deserves better."

"Let me show you how to make oatmeal." Kylie pushed her up to the counter. "I brought baby oatmeal, some fruit and the stuff that Ethan had in his truck. It's all here on top of the counter."

Eve nodded, not knowing what else to say. If only life could be lined up the way Kylie lined up ingredients for a perfect, healthy breakfast. If only Eve knew all of the right answers, the right choices to make. But she didn't, so she did the only thing she knew to do. She followed directions and made breakfast for Tori.

Voices raised in a heated discussion greeted Ethan as he made his way downstairs. He'd been in isolation since Tuesday, agreeing with Carson West, Jack's physician son, that it would be best if he waited until Thursday before venturing around others. No need to make Tori or any of the other ranch inhabitants sick. Not that he'd really met the others. He'd seen Jack and met Isaac and Carson, as well as Sierra.

"I'm telling you, Jack, I'm not a wedding planner or a caterer."

If Ethan had to guess, that very upset voice belonged to Sierra. The chuckle that came afterward probably was Jack's.

"Oh, Sierra, you're always so quick to doubt yourself," Jack responded. "I have more confidence in you than you've got in yourself."

"That's because you believe the best of everyone." Sierra's tone softened.

Ethan thought he should probably make himself known. He walked a little heavier, hoping they would hear him as he descended the stairs.

"That must be our patient." Jack's voice carried up the stairs.

"That must be my cue to leave," Sierra returned.

But she didn't leave. She was sitting at the kitchen island with a cup between her hands and a furrowed brow as if she had a million things on her mind.

"It looks as if I spared you all the plague," Ethan quipped as he entered the kitchen. "Jack, thank you for opening your home to me."

Jack waved off his thanks. He turned so that he could see both Ethan and Sierra.

"It's a pleasure having you here, Ethan." Jack nodded toward the coffeepot, his head jerking just a fraction as he made the gesture. "Help yourself to some coffee. And also to that room for as long as you need it."

"I appreciate that." Ethan headed for the coffeepot. "I'm also grateful for the coffee."

"Will you be staying around?" Sierra asked as she stood and carried her cup to the sink.

"I'm probably going to be in the area for a while. My family is starting a new farm implement business on the outskirts of Tulsa. I'll be managing it for the time being."

"Oh, so you'll be living in the area, then?" Sierra asked, a merry glint in her eyes.

"No. I'll get the business off the ground and then we'll hire a general manager."

"Leave him be, Sierra," Jack warned. "I only have four children but sometimes I feel like I have dozens."

Sierra's expression softened. She gave Jack an affectionate hug on her way out. "You do have dozens of children. And we all love you."

"Most of the time they love me."

"I love you all of the time," Sierra responded. "But I disagree with you often."

He waved her off and she left.

"Have a seat," Jack offered. "There are fixings for breakfast burritos in the warmers on the counter over there. During the week we keep things casual. Maria cooks up a meal and keeps it heating in the warmers. On weekends we have a big breakfast and whoever is available joins us. A few times a week we have what we refer to as family dinners. But you grew up on a working ranch, didn't you?"

"Yes, we have about a thousand acres. We still work cattle and raise horses but my mom also started a guesthouse on the ranch."

"A dude ranch?" Jack asked.

"No, more of a country bed-and-breakfast. It's an updated farmhouse that sat on about ten acres that adjoined our property. When it came up for sale, my mom bought it, put a pool in the backyard and turned it into her dream business."

"Now that's an idea I hadn't thought of. With this wedding venue, I wonder if I should consider a guesthouse for people who need a place to stay before or after the wedding."

"It's something to consider."

Jack arched a brow and a smile tugged at one corner of his mouth. "I can't wait to tell Sierra about your idea."

"Oh, please don't use my name. She's already positive I contaminated the entire ranch."

Jack looked forlornly into his empty coffee cup.

"Want me to get you another?" Ethan offered.

"Nah, I've had my cup for the day. Carson says I'm

not allowed to drink too much caffeine. You know, as a man ages, he ought to be able to have what he wants."

"It would seem that way," Ethan agreed.

"Well, anyway, no use lamenting what we can't change. I guess we have other things to discuss. Like if you're planning to take Eve away from us."

Ethan hadn't expected the question, and he definitely hadn't planned an answer. He sat there for a long moment trying to decide the best way to respond.

"I'm not sure," he admitted. "I kind of flew off the handle when I found out she was living here. I loaded Tori up in the car and headed this way without much of a plan."

"I can see how you might have been upset with her." Jack picked up the empty cup again. "But you gotta remember, it's a difficult thing, coming back from a war."

Ethan hadn't really thought about Eve's time in Afghanistan, what she'd seen, experienced, or what had led to her injury. It was as if she had lived a whole other life he knew nothing about. In truth, he didn't really know her anymore. He only knew that she'd been determined to serve her country and she'd done so against her parents' wishes.

"I'm sure it is difficult," he responded to Jack's statement about the war.

"Yes, to say the least. War changes a person. Takes away your innocence. It opens your eyes to the frailties of life. It exposes you to the very worst of humanity." Jack paused for a moment, as if searching for answers. "It also introduces you to the best of humanity and teaches you your own strengths and weaknesses."

Eve. Ethan had no doubt that Jack was giving him

insight without really mentioning what had happened to her.

"Jack, are you sure you wouldn't mind if I stay here for a while? I wouldn't mind paying for room and board. But I feel like Eve needs time to get to know Tori before she can make a decision."

"Of course you can stay here. The bedroom you've been using is yours for as long as you need it. As for Eve, she can be stubborn. I hope for the sake of that little girl that the two of you can come to some kind of understanding."

"Me, too." But he didn't know what was meant to happen or how this would all turn out.

They couldn't go backward in time, to what they had once meant to each other. But now they had Tori and a court date less than six weeks away.

He heard a low rumble on the ramp outside and then voices raised in animated discussion. Jack pushed the coffee cup to the far side of the counter, giving Ethan a conspiratorial wink as he did. The too-innocent look on the older man's face had Ethan wondering if maybe he wasn't supposed to have even one cup of coffee.

The door opened and Eve zoomed in followed by Sierra. Tori was sitting on Eve's lap, the band of fabric from the baby sling holding her in place.

"You survived," Eve said. Tori bounced on her lap, holding out her arms to Ethan. "And look who missed you. She's probably ready to head back to Texas."

No beating around the bush for Eve. Then he'd be straight with her, too.

"I'm not going anywhere."

Her eyes widened as she pushed her chair closer. "What?"

"Jack said I could stay here as long as needed. Between the new dealership and this situation with Tori, it will help if I'm close at hand."

"Close at hand?" She shook her head. "Ethan, I can't do this."

"I think you can, Eve."

"But how? You said we have to go to court in six weeks. The judge wants us to come up with a stable environment to raise Tori in. I live here. You live in Texas. I'm not in a position to be a mother."

"You think I was in a position to be a dad?"

"I don't know." She hesitated. "You know Tori. You've had time with her."

"Yes, I met her five times before that day I got a phone call from James's dad telling me about the accident and letting me know that Tori was in a foster home. I made a decision to get her and figure out what was the best thing for her. The lawyer made everything very real and legal. I'm sorry that you didn't have time to prepare for all this. We didn't have time either."

"I didn't mean it like that. I just…" Eve looked down and he knew where her mind was going. She was thinking about her weaknesses rather than her many strengths. But he didn't have the right to tell her what he thought. It'd been a long time since he'd had that right.

He knelt in front of her, aware that Sierra and Jack had left the room. "Look, I get it, we're over. But for Tori's sake, we have to figure something out. She deserves that, doesn't she? We owe it to her and to our friends."

"I know. I just…" She closed her eyes. "I'm afraid."

Eve had never been afraid of anything. She'd chased after her dreams, conquered obstacles. He touched his forehead to hers, wishing that he could take her in his arms and comfort her.

"I get that you're afraid, Eve. But I also know that you're strong. And I'm asking you to give us a month of your life. Help us figure out a plan."

"I'm not sure if I can do this."

He didn't argue with her but he thought he knew her better than she knew herself. Her arm circled Tori, protective, loving. Tori needed her. But maybe Eve had needed Tori, too.

And Ethan? He wasn't going to admit what he wanted or needed from this relationship. She'd not only broken his heart, she'd broken his trust.

He wasn't looking for another go-round of pain from the only woman he'd ever loved.

Chapter Five

"One month," Eve said, looking down at the baby in her arms and avoiding the man in front of her. It wouldn't be easy to keep her heart from connecting with Tori. And as much as she wanted to fight it, her heart was already linked to Ethan. He'd always been there, even though she thought she'd gotten over him.

For Tori, she could manage for a month. "I'll help you while you're here," she said, needing to set ground rules. "I will not move back to Texas. I just can't. While you're here, we will figure out a plan. We'll figure out this parenting thing together."

"A month. I'll take that." He stood and grabbed a seat at the counter. "I can use the help. I might seem like I have this all figured out but becoming a parent overnight hasn't been easy. There's a lot I don't know. There are times that she cries and I have no idea how to comfort her."

"And you think *I'm* going to have the answers?" She laughed. "Ethan, I never even had a babysitting job. My parents were in their early forties when I was born. For the first twenty years of their marriage, they were too busy being activists to have children. And all of their friends were older and childless."

"I still say you have a knack for this."

"Yeah, well, she's sweet and easy to love."

"I'm not sure what's going to happen with all this, Eve, but I can't give her over to strangers. I just can't imagine doing that. What are we supposed to do, walk in to a judge and say, 'Sorry, our best friends trusted us but we can't do this'?"

Eve didn't have answers.

"I'm not sure what we're supposed to do."

"I guess we take it one day at a time."

"I guess we will." She unwrapped the sling and lifted Tori, holding her out to Ethan. "That makes today your day. I have to catch up on a lot of work. I lost a couple of days."

"But I have to go to Tulsa."

"Then what do we do? What do you usually do with her when you're working? You didn't bring her to me just to have a free babysitter. Did you?"

"No, of course not." The words were spoken in an indignant tone but she thought he looked somewhat guilty. It might have been years but she still knew him well.

She laughed. "You did!"

"I didn't!" he protested, taking Tori from her. She immediately grinned and patted his cheeks. "Since the funeral we've been in a holding pattern. I haven't worked much and I've had my mom and Bethany to help. But I couldn't put off this trip to Tulsa and then Bethany saw your name in the article about Mercy Ranch."

"I'm sorry," she said. "You shouldn't have found me

that way. I should have called you a long time ago. I made a decision in the days following the accident."

Accident seemed like a vague description for what had happened to her overseas. The word *accident* implied something accidental, not planned, not orchestrated. Her heart thumped hard and fast as her mind took up the scattered memories of that day and tried to thread them together. She shook her head.

"Are you okay?" Ethan asked, his voice low, concerned.

"Fine. I'm fine. But the point is, I made a decision and acted on it. Later, after the dust settled, I should have called and explained. But by then, months had passed."

"Did you have second thoughts?" His gaze bored into her and she shook her head.

"No. I didn't have second thoughts." No second thoughts but a lot of regret. Were the two one and the same? "I did the right thing."

"For who?"

She blinked at the unexpected question. "For you, of course. So that you could find someone else and have everything you had always wanted."

"I wanted…" He let the words drift away as he settled Tori on his lap.

"I'm sorry." She'd been sorry since the day of the accident. Sorry for the lives lost. Sorry for herself. Sorry that she couldn't fix things and have the marriage they'd planned.

"Yeah, me, too. So, about Tori. I'm going to have to run to Tulsa in the next day or two."

"And you're not going to take her with you." It wasn't a question. "The problem is, I have work to do, too. I have a job. Two jobs, actually."

"Already fighting like a married couple," Sierra said as she entered the kitchen. She held her hands up. "Don't look at me. I'm not getting in the middle of this. And I'm certainly not a babysitter. Maybe the two of you could switch off. Not that communication seems to be your strong suit."

Her comment caused Ethan to bark with laughter. "That hits the nail on the head. Communicating might have resolved a lot of our problems."

"Communicating would have meant you trying to convince me that we would be fine, and me feeling as if I had trapped you into something you didn't sign up for."

"That's TMI. I'm heading to the chapel, and I'm not ever getting married." Sierra walked off singing the last line. "Just be glad you dodged the bullet, Ethan. Seriously. I've never seen a marriage that ended with a happy-ever-after."

"My parents have been married for forty years," he called after her as she walked out the back door.

"She can't be convinced. Her parents were a night-mare."

Tori started to fuss in his arms. Eve thought about reaching for her, but that would be a commitment. The two of them raising this child together. She really did want that. She wanted to comfort this baby girl, love her, cherish her. Because she was Hanna's. And because Eve really did love babies. She used to dream about the half dozen kids she and Ethan would have. They'd even named some of them. Because she'd grown up lonely, an only child. And he'd always dreamed of a big family.

"Let's take her back to the apartment and feed her. Maybe she's hungry?" Eve really didn't have a clue.

"She probably wants to get down and play." Ethan's suggestion made sense.

"I really don't know," Eve admitted. "I seriously don't know anything about kids, other than the two that belong to Carson and Kylie."

Eve turned toward the back door, confident that Ethan followed. As soon as they were in the open air, Tori stopped fussing.

"Did you think I would smother you?" Ethan asked as they crossed the wide expanse of lawn. "I mean really, I'm trying to understand how the person I planned to live my life with suddenly didn't trust me enough to tell me what had happened to her while serving overseas."

She'd never really thought about it from his perspective. Now she couldn't stop thinking about how she'd hurt him. There was some truth to the words. She knew that Ethan, like her parents, would have wanted to take care of her. She would have felt the same had something happened to him.

"After the accident, I was trying to figure out my new normal and how I would live the life I'd suddenly been handed. I wasn't thinking about your feelings. I was thinking about survival. About how it would feel to pull the rug out from under you, taking all of your dreams away."

He silently shook his head.

"What?"

"Nothing. Just nothing. I'm not sure what to say."

"Will you forgive me?"

He stepped in front of her, forcing her to stop. "I've forgiven you. But you were my best friend, the woman I loved and wanted to spend my life with. Obviously I must have wanted that more than you did."

Tori's bottom lip quivered.

"The two of you have to stop." Sierra approached them, her hazel eyes flashing with anger.

"Stop what?" Eve shook her head, confused.

Sierra stormed up to them. "Get over yourselves. Stop talking about the past and who got hurt the worst." She took Tori from Ethan's arms, her expression softening. "This baby is yours. You both have an obligation to give her a safe and loving environment. I'm not a relationship expert, but I do know how it feels to be this child. So stop. Not another word about what Eve did or why she did it or how it made you feel. Get over it. Love this baby. Be happy around her. Have fun with her. Have your grown-up discussions somewhere other than with her in your arms. Now, I have fifteen minutes to spare. Go take a walk. Hash it out. Tori and I are going inside. You're not welcome in there until you've figured out how to talk without making her sad."

Eve watched her friend walk away, whispering to Tori as she went. Slowly she turned to face Ethan. He brushed a hand through his hair and let out a long sigh.

"Parenting fail," she said.

"Big-time."

"I told you we're not cut out for this. Or maybe I'm not cut out for this. Do you know I've never seen my parents fight?" She ran her hands over the wheels of her chair. "We might have made a royal mess of our marriage. And our six kids would have been in serious trouble."

"Eve, my parents have one of the strongest relationships I know of. They sometimes disagree. In front of me and my sister. And they also work it out in front of us, too."

"But we made Tori cry." She started to roll past him.

"We have to talk," he said. "We have to get to a place of understanding."

"Right, of course we do." She could have told him she really wanted to run away from him, from this conversation. She didn't want to face anything. But the determined look in his eyes told her the time for running was over.

"Where do we go?" he asked.

She took off without giving an answer so he followed. And it didn't take him long to figure out their destination. She left the sidewalk and headed across the lawn. There were two options: the stable or the dog kennel. Because she'd always loved the stables back in Texas, he assumed that was their destination. He didn't know the protocol for helping her, or if she'd want help. He took hold of the handles of the wheelchair, just in case.

And he headed them in the direction of the stable.

Her gloved hands grabbed the wheels and stopped them.

"Ethan, would you ever pick me up and carry me where I didn't want to go?" she asked without looking back.

"No, I wouldn't." He backed away from the chair.

"Then don't take control of my chair unless I ask and don't think you can push me where I don't want to go."

"I'm sorry." He waited, knowing there was a lesson to be learned in this.

"This chair is a part of me, it's my legs. It's my freedom. I resented it at first, now I realize that it gets me where I want to go. It gives me independence."

"Got it." He lowered his hat to shade his face from the midmorning sun and stared down at the dark head that tilted, the chin jutting angrily. Oh, boy, she hadn't changed much at all. She'd always stood her ground. She didn't like to be pushed around. She said it was because her parents were political activists and had strong opinions. She'd learned early on to stand up for what she believed in. Even when what she believed in upset those very same parents.

"Why not the stable?" he asked, keeping his tone even.

"Because I don't want to go there. I just don't."

He got it. It was another place she avoided. The same way she avoided home, her family, her friends.

Her fiancé.

Ethan brushed a hand over his face.

"The dog kennel," she offered. "If you want to go with me to the dog kennel, we can talk there."

"Is that what most people call a compromise?" He grinned at her, and wonder of wonders, she smiled back.

"Yeah, I guess it is. I don't want to fight with you, Ethan. I definitely don't want to fight in front of Tori. I want to find a way that we can be friends."

He started to tell her that he'd always thought they were friends. In the spirit of compromise, he avoided that statement. "Can I help you across the rougher ground?"

"You can."

Friendship. With the woman he thought he'd spend the rest of his life with. It was ironic, really, that they were now joined in a union they wouldn't have envisioned. Rather than husband and wife, raising a family together, they were trying to find a way to co-exist. For Tori's sake.

They reached the dog kennel and he took a seat on

the bench. Eve opened a kennel and called the dog inside. The chocolate Labrador left the enclosure and sat next to her chair. She slid her hand down its head and the dog leaned into the caress.

He was jealous of the dog.

She finally looked up, her eyes soft, her expression thoughtful. "Well?"

She was the woman he'd fallen in love with. It hit him full force, like a fist to the solar plexus. She was smart, funny, caring, beautiful. He'd kissed her for the first time the night after she graduated high school. He'd kissed her for the last time when he put her on a plane, her destination an airbase that would take her to Afghanistan.

"Ethan?"

He cleared his throat, trying to pretend he'd been thinking about her question and their situation. Instead he'd been thinking about kissing her. He guessed his whole lecture to himself about not trusting her was one he hadn't taken to heart.

"Let's just take one day at a time for now. We've discussed it. Let's get on with life and figure it out as we go."

"I'm a planner."

"I know you are." He laughed at the memories. She'd designed their home, their ranch, given their six children names that were alphabetical. "Alexander, Benjamin, Cadence, Dusty, Eloise, Franny," he reminded her.

She laughed so hard she wiped away tears. "There just wasn't an F name that went with Forester."

"I know. I remember."

"I'm sorry for hurting you."

"I know."

She drifted for a moment. He watched as she scanned

the horizon, settling her gaze on horses grazing in a distant field.

"I don't want to hurt you again and I'm afraid I will. We've managed to move on and I'm afraid this will open up the wounds. It will hurt all over again. I do not want to go back to Texas and be someone that everyone takes care of. I can't. I won't."

He wanted to tell her that plenty of people went through difficult times and allowed their loved ones to help. It wasn't about being suffocated. It was about having people who cared.

She must have deciphered something in his look because she reached for his hand. "You would have."

"I wouldn't have meant to."

"I know that. Remember when you convinced my dad to sell my roan mare? You'd decided she was too much for me to handle."

"She tried to take you off under a barn door."

"If you'd given me time, I might have made that decision for myself. Instead you rushed in and made it for me."

"I only did it because I cared."

And he did still care about her. Very much.

"My parents drove me to every band competition, every barrel race. They wouldn't let me near a school bus. I get that buses can be dangerous but every other member of the band got to ride the bus. Same thing with school trips. I never had a sleepover at a friend's house, never went with a group to the movies or any of the other things that everyone else was doing."

"Their overprotectiveness went above and beyond."

"I wanted to serve my country so I joined the army,

because it was a place where they couldn't protect me."
She didn't cry but her eyes filled with tears. "I showed
them."

"Eve…" He didn't know what else to say.

Her hand tightened around his. He pulled off the
glove. He slid his fingers through hers, interlocking.
She looked up, confusion in her dark chocolate eyes.
Slowly he raised her hand and dropped a kiss on her
knuckles, allowing himself only that much contact. The
gesture was meant to comfort her. Instead it felt like a
cord being pulled tight between them.

She pulled her hand free, then touched his cheek, her
fingers lightly tracing a path to his jaw. Ever so slowly
she touched her lips to his. It was fleeting, and then the
moment was gone.

Afterward she smiled, looking pleased with herself.
"I've never kissed any man other than you."

He remained silent.

"And you're the only man I'll ever kiss. I want you
to know that. I didn't end our engagement in order to
find someone else. Or because I found someone else. I
ended it so that *you* could find someone."

"Am I supposed to say thank you?"

"It would be the polite thing to do," she teased. "I'm
sorry, that isn't funny. I know it hurt. I hope you understand that it hurt me, as well."

"And here I thought you were taking the easy way
out."

She moved back a few feet and closed the kennel,
keeping the chocolate Lab at her side. "Stay, Tex."

"I have to go to Tulsa tomorrow." He stood up, re-
alizing that maybe it was time to end this discussion.

"And you want me to take care of Tori?"

He shrugged, then waited for her response, not wanting to push.

"I can do that. I'm sure if I get in a bind, someone will help me out."

"Thank you. For being willing to watch her. I know this is an adjustment but I'm glad she has us both."

".I just want to make that clear. I'm not convinced I can take care of a baby. I've adjusted to my new reality. I know I've talked a lot about my independence and taking care of myself. What you need to realize is that it took a lot of time and work to get here. And it isn't easy. I still struggle."

"I can imagine."

"No, you can't, so I'll explain. I'm not looking for pity because I love my life. I just want you to have a clear understanding. This chair changes almost everything about how I live my life. How I take care of myself. How I get from place to place. There are days that I think about something I need to get and I realize that I can't climb the ladder to reach whatever is on the top shelf. I can't chase after a puppy that gets loose. I can't dance with you under the moonlight. Remember our crazy plan to have our reception outside under the stars?"

"I remember."

"Stop being so stinking nice," she lamented, her tone cross. The dog whined and moved closer to her side.

"Do you want me to tell you what I think? I think that you were selfish. You weren't thinking about me at all. I think you were considering how you would feel if I had to help you, care for you. You were thinking how mad it would make you if you had to ask me to climb that ladder for you. You were thinking I would want to dance and you couldn't. Maybe those are all valid points for you. You definitely didn't consider how I would feel if I lost you and didn't know why."

"I did think about you. But I'll admit that I thought about myself." She held up a hand. "No more arguing. James and Hanna left us the most important part of themselves. Now we have to think about Tori and what's best for her."

"I couldn't agree more." He handed her the glove he'd taken from her hand. "Just so you know, I would still dance with you under the stars."

"I need to feed the dogs." She changed the subject, moving away from him as she did.

"And I need to make phone calls. I'm going to call my parents."

Eve didn't respond to that. He noticed.

"I didn't say I expect *you* to call *your* parents."

He left her there because that's what he thought she'd want. She didn't want to be coddled. She wanted to take care of her animals and live the life she'd built for herself. He realized that by showing up here, he'd changed everything for her.

Finding her had changed everything for him. It remained to be seen what those changes would be.

But he knew one thing: nothing would ever be the same.

Chapter Six

From where she sat at her desk, Eve had a clear view of Glory and Tori. The teenager had long blond hair, a dress she'd made for herself from quilt pieces and a beaded necklace that Tori loved to grab. Glory had offered to help with Tori. They'd given it a test run the previous day, and decided today they would try an afternoon so that Eve could get some work done.

"So tell me again, why do you have this baby?" Glory asked as she spooned a bite of mashed banana into Tori's mouth.

It seemed that Glory had gotten clean and she'd gone all natural. She'd insisted on making her own baby food because at least she knew it had no additives. Glory reminded Eve of her own parents.

Glory watched her, clear blue eyes behind wire-framed glasses, waiting for Eve to answer her question. The girl had been at the apartment for only thirty minutes and so far she'd peppered her with every question imaginable. Why was Eve in a wheelchair? Did she think Joe was cute? Could she imagine being married to someone as nice as Dr. Carson West?

"Tori's parents were killed in a car accident," Eve answered while staring at her computer screen. Hopefully Glory would take the hint.

"That's tough. My own parents have both been in and out of jail my whole life. My dad was a drug dealer. People wonder why I turned out the way I did. I mean, it doesn't take a genius to figure it out. But at least I'm trying to get my act together. What is your job?"

"I translate documents." Eve reached for her headphones.

"Is that hard? I mean, you obviously have to be able to speak other languages."

"I speak Arabic and Spanish." Eve supplied the information, thinking to head off the next question.

"Wow. You're smart. I wish I was smart."

Eve sat back from her computer. "How do you know you're not smart?"

"Because I've never been good at school."

Eve watched as Glory finished feeding Tori. The teen picked up the baby, wiped her face, kissed her cheek and then held her close. A look of longing spread across the pale face of the young mother whose own child was living with Kylie and Carson.

"You know, being good at school is great," Eve said, thinking about the best response. "Some people are super smart and yet they struggled in school. Would you like to take a test? Maybe we can figure out what you're good at and you can start taking classes. It helps to know where your strengths are. I'm good at languages but really struggle in science."

"Really?" Glory sat down in a chair next to Eve, still holding Tori.

Obviously she wouldn't be getting any work done today. But Glory's expression had gone from defeated to hopeful, so working a few extra hours during the evening didn't seem like such a bad thing. She exited her program and searched for an online aptitude test. When she found it, she pushed back from the desk and reached for Tori.

"Let's try this test. Don't worry or get stressed, it's just for fun."

"What do I do?" Glory looked from Eve to the computer.

"Select the correct answer on each question. Simple as that. If you need paper, there's a notebook and a pencil in the top drawer of my desk."

"What about Tori?"

"I can handle Tori for thirty minutes. Think of this as fun, as a challenge."

Glory bit down on her bottom lip but she nodded. "Okay, I can do this."

"You can. Tori and I are going to check to take Tex for a walk." At the mention of his name, the chocolate Lab perked up. He'd been resting on the floor next to her chair but he moved to her side, ears perked.

Eve wrapped the baby sling around Tori.

"What if I mess up?" Glory stared at the computer. "I'm not good at these things."

"This test isn't one you can mess up." Eve moved a little closer to the teen. "Glory, you're smart. If you weren't smart you wouldn't have survived your childhood. You wouldn't be working this hard to get your child back. Yeah, you've struggled, but that doesn't mean you can't learn and it doesn't mean you don't have skills or gifts."

"Okay, I'll try."

"Of course you will. I'll be back."

Eve glanced back as she went out the door of the apartment. Glory was leaning over the computer, a mask of concentration on her face. Just as Eve closed the door, the teen smiled and her eyes widened.

Kylie was coming up the sidewalk as Eve left the apartment.

Tex started toward her. Eve gave him a command and he returned to her side. She could see in Kylie's eyes that she wanted to pet the animal. And, of course, Tex sensed he had a friend in her. It was a challenge, to teach a dog to refrain from seeking attention from every friendly human they encountered. In public she used a harness with the warning that he was in training and please, don't touch. Of course, small children often ignored the warning. And she understood. Tex was a big brown teddy bear of a dog.

"Where are you going?" Kylie asked.

"Tori and I are giving Glory a little time. She's taking a test."

"A test?" Together they walked toward the kennel.

"Aptitude test," Eve explained. "She doesn't think too highly of herself. I thought it might help. And it will also give her a list of strengths and career options."

"I hadn't thought about that."

"Because you're too close to the situation," Eve answered. She had to stop and adjust Tori, who struggled to get free of the sling.

"Want me to take her?" Kylie offered.

Eve accepted. "Please. She gets tired of being confined."

"You're doing really well with her."

"For two whole days I've managed to keep her safe and keep my sanity." Eve didn't think that qualified as a win.

"Are you looking for a reason to doubt yourself?"

"Not at all, just being realistic. I'm sorry, I think it's lack of sleep talking." As if on cue, Eve yawned. "I've also been wondering when Ethan will get back from Tulsa."

"Have you talked to him?"

"Yesterday."

"How'd that go?" Kylie asked as they headed toward the main house.

"It's awkward," Eve admitted. "I hurt him. And now I have to live with the consequences."

"Yes, you do." Kylie kissed Tori on the cheek. "But we've discussed that more than once. It is about the past, but it's also about the choices you make for the future."

"I've got a lot to think about in the next few weeks. I'm pretty sure Ethan isn't going to just go away. He wants me to be a part of the decision-making process for Tori."

"And you should be part of that process. Your friends trusted you."

"What were they thinking?" She met Kylie's sympathetic gaze.

"They were thinking that if they weren't here to raise Tori, they wanted someone who would love her the way they loved her. And you're thinking that they should have picked someone else. Maybe they knew you better than you knew yourself."

"Hanna knew about the accident. I made her promise not to tell Ethan."

Kylie's eyes widened. "Wait a second. They knew the two of you weren't married? Hanna knew about your accident?"

"Don't."

"Don't what?" Kylie tried to look innocent.

"Do not think that this is a 'meant to be' moment. This is…"

"Complicated?" Kylie offered.

"Very. Especially since my thoughts on marriage haven't changed."

Kylie shifted Tori to one arm. Without warning, she leaned and hugged Eve. "I am sorry. And I'm praying for you, for Tori and for Ethan. You know I won't lecture you. We all have different paths and we have to make our own choices."

They reached the ramp that led to the back door of Jack's house. Kylie sat Tori in her lap. The baby looked at Eve and started crying, with big tears rolling down her cheeks.

"She doesn't even like me."

"Oh, please, that has nothing to do with it. She's been jostled around, left with people she doesn't know, adjusted to a new schedule and a new bed."

"Exactly, she has a schedule, a person she trusts. She's smart enough to know that I am not her person. And I'm not the person Ethan expects me to be. Every time he looks at me, I can tell he's looking for the girl he used to know. She isn't in here."

"I love you but sometimes you're the most stubborn person I know," Kylie said without a smile.

Eve returned the serious look. "Ditto."

"I have this friend who works out every day. She cooks. She trains service dogs for veterans. She handles an at-home job. And yet she doesn't believe in herself."

"Sounds interesting." Eve hooked an arm around Tori and managed to move her chair a few feet. "I hope Maria has coffee on."

"I'm sure she does. And Jack brought home a rhubarb pie from Holly's. You know she's officially changed the name of the café to Holly's? The sign went up yesterday."

"I didn't know that. I'm so happy for her. I hope she doesn't get too exhausted, trying to take care of the café and her mother."

"I know," Kylie agreed. "I worry about her."

She pulled the door open and pushed Eve through the entrance into the back sunporch and through to the dining room and kitchen.

"I worry about her, too. I don't know her story as well as you do, but I do know that she struggles to keep her mom healthy."

The aroma of fresh-brewed coffee wafted from the kitchen to greet them. And the sound of voices raised in a less-than-happy discussion.

"Surely you can find someone else," Sierra was saying, sounding like she was at the end of her rope.

"Do you think we should leave?" Eve whispered to Kylie.

"No, we might have to intervene. Jack is getting

pretty good at digging in his heels and not backing down. Sierra is a match for anyone."

They entered the kitchen and Eve managed to plaster an "I didn't hear anything" look on her face. She glanced up at her friend and smiled because Kylie's expression wasn't as serene as she probably thought.

"Jack, how's that new cutting horse that Isaac bought?" Kylie asked.

"He's a dandy," Jack stated, still glowering at Sierra. "I think he's world-champion material. But you know how Isaac is. He'll decide to make the animal into a kid's horse and give pony rides at fairs."

"I doubt that," Kylie shot back. "He's taking horses to Wyoming for a rodeo, isn't he?"

"Yeah, next month. Rebecca and Allie are going with him. It'll be quiet with them away from the ranch."

"Yes, I'm sure it will be," Kylie agreed. "Is there any of that pie left?"

"It's on the counter," Sierra said. "Would you please explain to Jack that I'm not a wedding planner, and I definitely don't want the new minister showing up here every other week telling me what I need to do? He does enough of that on Sundays."

Eve hugged Tori tight. "This is home, sweetie. For better or worse."

"Don't say 'for better or worse' in my presence," Sierra grumbled. "I'm going to be hearing enough of that when we start having weddings. And you'd better watch yourself. Jack might have you heading down the aisle before anyone else. Right, Jack?"

Jack sputtered a bit, and before he could comment, Sierra headed for the back door.

Eve watched her friend through the window as she headed back across the yard. Then she ignored Jack and headed for the coffeepot. She did not have a wedding in her future.

Ethan glanced at the clock on the dash of his truck. He'd planned on being back in Hope earlier in the day but he'd gotten busy, and then he'd made a quick call to the Realtor who had sold them the land for their Tulsa business. That appointment had taken him longer than he'd intended. But with good results.

Or at least he thought they were good. Eve might see things in a completely different light.

As he entered the city limits of Hope, he was taken in by the silence of the community. It was a town of less than a thousand people and the economy was supported by local business, most of which had been revived with the help of Jack West's philanthropy.

The café that had been Mattie's a few days prior now sported a big new sign. Holly's. He considered driving on past the café but it was dinnertime and he didn't want to show up at the West ranch looking for food.

He also wasn't quite ready to face Eve. He especially didn't want to tell her about the property twenty minutes west of Hope. He pulled in to a parking space and got out of his truck. Then he noticed a crowd of men walking up the sidewalk. A couple of them looked familiar. One of them waved at him.

"You're just in time for Friday 'all you can eat catfish'" the man called out as Ethan approached their group. Joe, Ethan thought his name was. He seemed to be a foreman at the ranch.

He was a big guy with a shaved head and a goatee. One side of his face was scarred and his right arm had been amputated.

"I'm always up for fried fish," Ethan responded, accepting the hand the other man held out. "Joe, right?"

"Joe Chapman. It's a good thing you're here. Maria over at the ranch caught your stomach virus and she's not cooking tonight. She's also not singing your praises."

"I was afraid of that." Ethan followed the group of ranch hands into the café. "I hope Jack doesn't get it."

"Jack moved to Carson's for a few days, just to make sure." Joe made his way through the café, greeting locals and shaking a few hands. "We're taking over the back room tonight since there are so many of us."

He headed in that direction, and Ethan fell in behind him. Up ahead, through the open door of the back dining area, he could see Isaac West, his fiancée and her daughter, Allie. Sierra, the reluctant wedding planner, was there, as well. And Eve. She sat at the end of the table with Tori in a high chair next to her. When she spotted him, her eyes narrowed.

Tori's reaction was much more favorable. The baby lit up, her eyes crinkling as she grinned big. She pounded on the high chair and jabbered a greeting. He hadn't been separated from her for this long since her parents' accident and it took him by surprise that he'd missed her. As unexpected as she'd been, he cared. Of course he cared. Maybe he had doubts from time to time but he knew deep down that he could do this. He had to do this.

"Look what the cat dragged back to town," Eve said as he took the seat next to her. "I was starting to think you weren't coming back."

He arched a brow at that. If anyone could be accused of running, it would be her. From the pink that highlighted her cheeks, he guessed she knew that already.

"I told you I would be back. I always keep my word." He picked up a spoon and gave Tori a bite of the green mush on the plate in front of her. "What is this?"

"Glory made it," Eve supplied. "She said organic homemade is better."

"Seems legit to me." He gave Tori another bite. "And she likes it."

"She mixed fruit with it. To give it flavor. Taste it, it's pretty good."

"I think I'll pass." But he did lift the spoon to his nose and smelled the concoction.

"Did you accomplish a lot?" Eve asked as they waited for the waitress to make her way to their end of the table.

"Yes, I did. More than I'd planned." He didn't really know what he'd planned with the property he had made an offer on. It had felt right and he'd seen potential in the house and the land. If things didn't work out, he knew it had decent resale value.

It had taken his parents by surprise. He'd called them and they'd discussed the options. In the end they'd understood and even encouraged him to figure out what he needed to do. For himself and for Tori.

"All-you-can-eat fried fish, or something off the menu?" the waitress asked when she reached him.

"Do the fish," Eve whispered.

"I'd planned on it."

The waitress wrote down his order. "Sweet tea to drink?"

Eve shot him a look. "Sure. Sweet tea."

Eve ordered next. Of course she ordered fried fish and sweet tea. The waitress scribbled the order on her order pad and hurried off.

"Not that I hadn't planned on ordering fish, but is there a reason you were so adamant about it?" he asked.

Eve gave Tori another spoonful of the vegetables, talking to her in sweet tones that took him by surprise. He knew her intention was to tell him she couldn't help raise Tori. But he hoped, prayed actually, that she'd change her mind. He couldn't imagine anyone spending time with Tori and refusing to raise her.

"Ordering fish makes things easier on Holly," she finally answered. "It's busy on fish night and we all try to stick with the special."

Conversation picked up at the table. Ethan observed as the men and Sierra discussed the workings of the ranch and the coming tourist and fishing season, as well as the wedding venue.

"I'm the last person who ought to be selling people dreams about happy-ever-after," Sierra groused. "It's going to be all white lace and pearls, sugary icing and glittery lights. The whole idea makes me cringe."

"Because you want everything draped in black?" Joe teased.

"I didn't say that," Sierra shot back. "But people ought to know that life doesn't get wrapped up with a pretty bow just because you meet someone and fall in love. Look at Isaac and Rebecca."

"I'll have you to know that we're very happy," Isaac countered. "Keep your negative sentiments to yourself."

"Not negative, honest. Marriage doesn't mean suddenly everything is perfect."

"True," Rebecca, Isaac's fiancée, responded. "A good marriage takes work from both people. It's a partnership. That doesn't mean there won't be difficult times to work through."

Sierra rolled her eyes and directed her cynical gaze in the direction of Ethan and Eve. Eve pointed at her.

"Do not start," Eve warned. "We all know your opinions on weddings. But Jack isn't asking you to get married. He knows you're a great businesswoman and he's asking you to manage a business. Separate your emotions from the wedding aspect and think of it as a business that you can manage and excel at."

Sierra pursed her lips. "I never thought of it that way."

"Exactly. Now, stop complaining."

Their dinners arrived and everyone was quiet as they ate Holly's amazing food. After the plates were cleared, people started to leave. Ethan lifted Tori from the high chair as Eve put the lid back on the container of baby food and dropped the empty container, bottle and toy into the bag on the side of her chair.

"Where did Sierra go?"

He looked around. "I don't know. I thought she went to pay for her meal but she never came back."

"Oh, she's truly gone too far. She brought me and Tori. She has the car seat."

"Is that a real problem?"

"It is a little bit of a problem. Babies require car seats. I'm not an expert but even I know that. And I require a car that I can get in and out of."

"I'm sure we'll manage. But maybe she's waiting out front?"

She shook her head. "Nope. I know her too well. Miss Jaded-and-Angry doesn't believe in happy-ever-after, but she doesn't mind meddling in other peoples' lives. Which is why Jack gave her the ranch's wedding venue to manage."

"Giving you a ride home shouldn't upset our lives that much. Let me pay and we'll see what we can do."

He left her sitting at the table trying to figure out how she'd lost control of her life. He knew her well enough to know that's where her thoughts would go.

His own were not quite as dire. As much as he didn't want to trust Eve, he found himself returning to the relationship they'd always had and the woman he'd always known. She had changed. She had gone through things that no one should have to endure. But she was still Eve.

She was still the woman he had loved. The woman he had wanted to spend his life with. No matter what obstacles she threw in his path or how much she tried to convince him that everything had changed, he knew better.

She was a determined woman, always had been. She was going to find that he was just as determined.

Chapter Seven

Twilight had descended, and as they left the café, Eve took a deep breath of late spring air. She could smell a hint of rain. That would make the farmers happy. They hadn't had rain in a week and they needed it for a good hay crop. All of those thoughts didn't draw her attention from the man pushing her wheelchair down the sidewalk.

"This is a pretty little town," he said as they approached his truck.

She nodded, agreeing with him. A few blocks away she could see the setting sun glimmering on the lake. The sky was painted shades of gray, blue, pink and lavender. Across the street she could see Rebecca, Isaac and Allie in the salon and day spa that Rebecca had come to Hope to start. It had been a rocky start, but the two of them together were a winning team.

When they reached his truck, she looked up at the behemoth of a vehicle. She'd spent her life not being overwhelmed or put off by anything. But from her vantage point in the chair, some things did overwhelm. Things she'd done without thinking about them now required careful thought, real planning.

And this truck, it was a giant.

And there was the car seat situation.

"Looks like she put the car seat in the back of my truck," Ethan noted as he reached into the bed of the truck for the seat. He put it in the backseat of his truck, secured it and turned to Eve.

She felt her breath hitch as they made eye contact. His dark eyes were shadowed beneath his hat, and his beard scruff took away the smooth handsomeness and turned him into a rugged cowboy. The cowboy she'd fallen in love with. The man she'd planned to marry.

She shook her head, freeing herself from those thoughts. She couldn't love him. She wouldn't. Neither of them needed complications from the past tangled up in the present.

"I'll get her," Ethan offered.

She started to say that they didn't really have another option but she refrained. She refused to be the bitter shrew who took her resentment of her situation out on the people around her.

She saved most of her resentment for quiet, private conversations with God.

Ethan lifted Tori from her lap. The baby had started to fall asleep and probably would have been sound asleep if they'd taken a longer walk.

Ethan finished buckling Tori into the seat. Then looked at Eve, then his truck. She sighed, because this was exactly what she'd wanted to avoid. That feeling of helplessness.

She could almost hear Kylie's voice. *Asking for help doesn't make a person helpless.*

"Tell me what to do," Ethan said matter-of-factly.

She focused on his eyes, searching for pity. The emotion wasn't there. That was a point in his favor.

"I would normally transfer myself but this truck is so tall, it's not an option."

"I can sell it."

She laughed at the offer. "Keep your truck, Ethan. You'll just have to pick me up and put me in the seat."

An apology for the situation almost slipped out but she bit it back. She couldn't apologize every time she needed help. But she could thank the person who helped her and be grateful.

"Any special way I should lift you?" His question brought her back to the present.

"I'll put my arms around your neck, then you lift me. I'm warning you, I'm not light."

"You're not heavy," he countered.

"Suit yourself, cowboy."

He leaned down and she wrapped her arms around his neck. She closed her eyes, swamped by emotions she'd so neatly boxed up and put away years ago, as if they'd never been apart. His scent, the feel of his strong muscles, the way his breath brushed her cheek, smelling of cinnamon. It would have been extremely uncomfortable had she not heard the catch in his breathing, as if he too felt the long-lost past twining between them.

After a brief pause he lifted her, holding her for a moment longer than necessary. They stood there between the door and his truck, sandwiched into a space barely big enough for the two of them.

"This is interesting," he finally said.

His face hovered just inches from hers. Their mouths were far too close. Her fingers itched to stray into his hair, perhaps to pull the cowboy hat off his head.

"This is dangerous," she responded.

"Maybe." He touched his forehead to hers and breathed deep. She did the same.

Then he placed her in the truck's passenger seat. He didn't ask permission, he just buckled her in. Afterward he gently splayed his right hand across her cheek and turned her to face him.

"Don't," she whispered. Her heart couldn't take another of his sweet, gentle kisses.

"Don't kiss you?"

She nodded because she found it impossible to speak.

His hands slid from her cheek and he backed away. "I won't. *This* time."

He closed the door. She watched in the rearview mirror as he folded her wheelchair and placed it in the bed of the truck. She watched as he rounded the truck and got in next to her. He started the truck and backed out of the space.

"How'd you and Tori do while I was gone?" he asked as the truck moved forward.

"We survived," she admitted. "Didn't get a lot of sleep but we survived."

Five miles of silence followed. He drove through the gates of the ranch and parked under the carport next to the apartment. They sat in silence, although it wasn't uncomfortable. Tori had fallen asleep. There were lights on in the apartment. A living room lamp and the light over the kitchen sink. If Sierra was home she must have gone into her own suite. Another quiet, lonely night.

Unless she had Tori. But if she took Tori to the apartment with her, that was another night of getting attached, another night of bonding. And where did it all end?

"Where do you see this going for us?" she asked as the sky darkened and the sun disappeared over the western horizon. Lights came on in the stable. The men were working in the arena.

She missed horses, sometimes so much she could cry.

"Is there an us?" he asked with a hint of a smile.

"No, there isn't," she clarified. "But there is Tori and that changes things."

"I see us raising her together," he admitted. He held her gaze and she knew she'd be the first to look away.

From where they sat, she could watch the outdoor arena. The lights were on, making the area as bright as day. They were team roping. Jack loved the sport. He said it fostered trust and teamwork.

Even from the inside of the truck, she could hear the shouts of the men, the noises of the steers in the pen. Sometimes they still got angry. She watched as one of the newer residents, Gabe, rushed at Joe. Joe shook his head and backed away. No one really had the courage to fight Joe. He was a wall of solid muscle, the black sheep in his US senator father's family.

Joe wasn't respectable, not the way his dad had intended. And he wasn't a fighter.

"It's quite a place, Mercy Ranch," Ethan spoke again. "I can see why you want to be here. Would you ever consider leaving?"

"I don't know."

She'd considered it. More than once. It was her safe place but that didn't mean it was her forever home. She thought about missing Jack, Kylie, Isaac, Joe and the others. She would miss her dogs. When he'd founded Mercy Ranch, Jack had bought the Labradors and the Labradoodle mix dogs to give them something to work with, something to focus on. Like the horses, the cattle and the other projects. Jack was of the opinion that busy hands kept a person focused on something that moved them forward. Isaac had been a kid when he got dumped at Mercy Ranch with the dad he'd never met. Back then Jack had been a mean drunk, his ranch on the verge of ruin, and Isaac had been his reason to keep going. He'd focused on giving his son a new life.

"How do you propose we raise Tori together?" Eve asked, going back to their previous conversation.

"As a couple."

She laughed. And then she saw that he was serious. Very serious.

That went as well as he had expected. He hadn't expected her to laugh in his face. But on a positive note, she hadn't punched him. Or screamed or told him to get out of the truck. Of course, it was his truck.

"You're kidding," she finally said after staring at him as if he'd just told her he was an alien.

"Not really. I do not want to lose Tori. I know it's crazy but I already feel as if she's mine. She's got me wrapped around her little finger. Maybe in time James and Hanna would have changed their will. Maybe they should have picked someone else. But they didn't. Even after you ended our engagement. Even though they didn't know where you were, they kept us as guardians of their child. I'm not going to let them down."

"Hanna knew about the accident," she said, looking away as she made the confession. At first he thought he'd misheard her.

"What?"

"I called her. I told her I couldn't marry you. She tried to talk me out of my decision. She told me to talk to you. But I knew if I talked to you, I would let you convince me you could handle it."

"Because I *can* handle it."

"You don't know that. You've been here less than a week. You have no idea. In the beginning there were days I wondered if I could handle it."

"We can handle it."

Her bullish expression shut him out. She shook her head and reached for the door handle. "*I* can. *We* can't. Please get my chair. It's really hard to make an exit when you can't even get yourself out of a truck."

"I'm sorry."

"Don't apologize."

He got out of his truck. The night air was humid, heavy with the hint of rain and the smell of dust and cattle. He grabbed the chair out of the back of his truck. He didn't know all of the ins and outs of how it had changed her life, how it would have affected his, but logically he knew she had valid reasons for what she'd done.

The four years he'd spent wondering, resenting her, all seemed pointless now that he knew her situation. Hanna had known. She'd never let on. But then, after getting married, Hanna and James had moved to the

Dallas area and he hadn't seen them as often as he would have liked.

The truck door opened. Eve glanced back at him, waiting impatiently for him to help her. He leaned in and her arms reached around his neck. She held tight as he lifted her from the truck. He held her a moment longer than she would have liked but he couldn't seem to find the moral character he'd always prided himself on. It'd gone missing along with pieces of his common sense.

"What are you doing?" she asked, outraged. Because he wasn't putting her in the chair. He wasn't letting her go so easily, not this time.

He leaned against the side of the truck, holding her in his arms. She wasn't as heavy as she'd warned.

"I should have hunted you down."

"What?"

"When you called and ended our engagement. I should have known something was wrong. The person I was in love with wouldn't have ended our engagement without a very valid reason. I allowed myself to believe you'd changed your mind. I let myself think that you'd picked the army—or another man—over us."

"I picked myself over us."

"What does that mean?"

"The horse. I kept thinking about that horse and how you convinced my dad I couldn't handle it and that it had to be sold. I pictured a lifetime of you telling me what I could and couldn't handle. I won't live that life. Not with you. Not with anyone."

"I wouldn't ask you to."

"You wouldn't ask. You would just make decisions. Because you like to protect. You want to take care of the people in your life. And right now, you're holding me, literally, against my will."

Until that moment he had considered kissing her. But her accusation made him realize what he'd done to her. Without further conversation, he settled her in her chair. She ignored him, grabbing gloves out of her side bag.

"I'll keep Tori with me tonight."

"Thank you." She turned to face him, peering up in the relative darkness. "Tori is a gift, Ethan. She's such a part of James and Hanna that it breaks my heart to look at her sometimes. I wish I had more faith in myself. More faith in general. I wish I understood how something like this happens to people, to a couple who loved each other, loved their daughter, loved God."

"It's a question everyone asks, Eve, not just you. It doesn't mean you've lost faith."

"I haven't lost faith," she admitted. "I'm just so angry sometimes that it scares me."

In the dark he could see the pain in her expression, the anguish in her dark eyes. He wanted to know more about her accident, her broken faith, about what had happened in Afghanistan.

The words were on his lips, that he understood. But he didn't say them.

"I think the correct thing to say would be that you have a right to be angry."

She smiled at that. "Thank you. Maybe someday…"

"You'll tell me?"

"Yes. Maybe."

He accepted that slight opening of a door, letting him back into her life. Maybe someday.

As he carefully gathered Tori out of the car seat, he

watched Eve make her way back to the apartment. The door opened before she got there, letting light spill out on the concrete front patio. Voices carried, hers and Sierra's, but he couldn't tell what they were saying to one another. Then the door closed.

"Tori, I'm a fool." He kissed the baby's cheek. She blinked, waking up from her nap.

With Tori in his arms, he headed for the arena, where the men were still team roping but had switched to a roping machine pulled by a four-wheeler. The replica steer had horns and hind legs for the riders to practice on. Joe drove the ATV around the arena and the two riders positioned behind it practiced lassoing the horns or the back legs. Tori squealed as they watched the horses work with the cowboys.

Not that it was all fun and games. A few of the horses balked at the idea of getting close to the mechanical steer. The replica squeaked and bounced as it was pulled across the arena. A cowboy on a pretty buckskin mare just about got tossed in the dirt when he allowed the horse to shy away from the steer.

"You need to push him back in and hold him," Ethan called out. "You're not in control of your horse and your legs are too loose. Use your legs."

Joe stopped the four-wheeler and pushed his hat back. "Finally, someone who knows what they're doing. Isaac was supposed to help out but he went and got himself engaged."

There were a half dozen men standing around. They appeared to range in age from about twenty to several years older than Ethan's thirty-one years.

"I can give some pointers," Ethan offered. "First, keep on that steer. And don't let your horse take control."

"Can you stick around?" Joe asked, firing the four-wheeler back up.

"Sure, for a bit."

Ethan moved to the risers where the men who weren't riding had taken seats to watch the others. He sat by a skinny young man with light-colored hair beneath his too-big hat and an easy smile.

"Hi, I'm Ethan."

"Kenny." The young man held out a hand. "I wasn't in the army."

"No?" Ethan asked but he watched the action in the arena.

"Nah, I couldn't join. Juvenile record. But I met Jack in Tulsa and he took me in. Probably a good thing. I would have ended up in prison."

Ethan gave the kid a longer look and he saw more. He saw that Kenny had a scar on his neck and other smaller scars on his face.

"Car accident," Kenny informed him without Ethan asking the question.

A truck started in the distance. The men sitting on the metal bleachers all looked toward the main house where the vehicle was backing out of the garage. Jack's truck, Ethan knew from his short stay at the ranch. But he thought Jack had temporarily moved to his son Carson's house.

"Isaac must be going to pick Jack up." Kenny supplied the answer. "Sometimes they get a call in the night from a veteran who needs a place to stay. The ranch is famous because of all the articles written about it. Jack only wishes he had more resources and could take in more people. He can handle about a dozen at a time. But most of them move on after they get their life together. Jack has a van and a driver to make sure they make it to VA appointments. He also acts as an advocate, making sure they get the care they need."

"He's quite a guy," Ethan agreed. Not many people would take their personal fortune and use it the way Jack West had used his.

"I owe him my life. Literally. He saw me in trouble, stopped his truck and physically put me in the backseat." Kenny shook his head. "No one ever cared whether I lived or died until Jack came along."

The words shook Ethan. He'd lived a fairly comfortable life on his family ranch. Sure, they'd had drought years, times when cattle prices tanked or instances when they'd had to borrow from the bank to keep things afloat, but he'd never really known hardship. Not really. He'd known heartache, but not hardship.

"It's a good thing there are people like Jack around," Ethan told Kenny. "And I'm glad he was there to help you out."

"Yeah, me, too. I'm going to college. Physical therapy. Crazy, right? Jack wants me to work here on the ranch. He said I have a gift because I help some of the guys with their PT."

"That's pretty impressive."

Kenny gave Tori a long look, his eyes narrowing. "Is she okay?"

The baby girl had been resting in his arms but as he looked down at her, her flushed cheeks indicated that she might have a fever.

"Kenny, I look forward to getting to know you better, but I think I'd better get her to the house."

"If you need anything, Dr. West's number is on the fridge," he said.

"Thank you." Ethan climbed down from the risers and headed for the house. Tori whimpered a little in her sleep. He considered waking Eve but then thought better of it.

Chapter Eight

Although Tori had been in Eve's life for less than a week, it seemed strange to sit at the kitchen table on Sunday morning and not have the baby with her. She had gotten up extra early, made coffee and toast. All the while she'd thought about the quiet apartment and how the baby changed everything.

When she heard footsteps, she expected it to be Sierra. Instead it was a woman close to Eve's age with short blond hair and bangs that hung across half her face, not really hiding a black eye.

"Oh, hi." The woman stopped mid-step and glanced around, as if seeking escape.

"New roommate?" Eve asked with a smile. Four years of roommates had taught her that each woman who arrived at Mercy Ranch had a story. This woman's story was written on the side of her face, and it wasn't a happy story.

"Yes, I guess I am. It was late when I got here. I'm glad I didn't wake you up."

"You didn't. I made coffee and there's toast. I'm not much of a cook."

"Thank you."

Eve poured herself a cup of coffee, giving the other woman a much-needed moment to compose herself. She heard the sniffle, then the paper towel being ripped off the roll.

"I'm Eve, by the way," she said as she turned her chair with one hand, holding the coffee with the other. It was a dangerous maneuver with hot liquid but she was confident.

"Abby Wallis," the other woman responded. "And I'm a mess. Sorry. I just never expected this. We were going to get married and then…he changed."

"I'm sorry," Eve responded, unsure of what else to say. It dawned on her that people did the same to her. They apologized because they didn't know how to respond. "You know what? Today, just try to get your bearings and if you need anything, ask."

"Is there a church nearby? Stupid question. Of course there is. This is Mercy Ranch."

"Yes, it is Mercy Ranch. I leave for church in an hour if you'd like to go."

Abby poured herself a cup of coffee and held the mug as if it were life support. "Yes, I'd like to go. I haven't been in years."

"You're welcome to ride with me."

"You drive?" Abby closed her eyes and gave her head a quick shake. "I'm sorry, of course you do."

"Don't be sorry, it was a valid question. I do have a car and yes, I drive. And usually safely."

"Usually?" Sierra appeared a few seconds later.

"Most of the time she thinks she's a race car driver. I would offer you a ride but I don't go to church."

"Oh, okay." Abby looked from Sierra to Eve.

Sierra breezed into the kitchen, her sundress swishing around her ankles. "Don't look so worried, I'm joking. Except for the part about church. Eve is the safest driver of us all. And the best person to hang out with. Speaking of which, I just saw Glory coming up the sidewalk. Let me guess, you've not only taken Tori to raise, but Glory, too? What's gotten into you?"

"She's lonely," Eve defended. Glory had called her two hours ago, asking if she could go to church with Eve. She would've gone with Carson and Kylie, but they had their children. And Cara. The girl had barely gotten her daughter's name out and started to cry.

"Of course she is. So are all of the dogs in the kennel. I'm surprised they're not all in the apartment with us." Sierra opened the fridge and pulled out a dozen eggs. "Abby, how did you sleep?"

"Not great but definitely better than I've been sleeping. Thank you for making this possible for me, Sierra."

"Don't thank me. Jack made the decision. But I do hope this gives you a place to start over."

A knock on the door signaled Glory's arrival. Sierra shouted for her to come in. Glory's blond hair hung loose in spiral curls and she wore a peasant skirt and T-shirt. Her wire-framed glasses appeared too big for her face.

"Glory, I'm glad you're here. Sierra was just starting omelets." Eve smiled at Abby. "Want one?"

Abby seemed to be a decent coconspirator. "I'd love an omelet, if we have time."

"Vegetables only," Glory said, her cheeks turning pink as she made eye contact with Sierra. "I'm trying a vegetarian diet."

"You need protein," Sierra shot back.

"I'm eating beans and nuts." Glory smiled sweetly, maybe not sincerely. "And eggs."

An hour later Eve pulled into the church parking lot. Glory jumped out immediately, having spotted Carson, Kylie and their children. She paused long enough to ask Eve if she needed help.

"I'm good, but thank you for asking. Go kiss Cara."

Abby waited, her short hair brushed to the side, covering her bruised and battered face. She pulled a pair of sunglasses out of her bag and slid them on.

"I never thought I would be *that* woman." She said when she noticed the direction of Eve's gaze. "I'm not even his wife, just his girlfriend. We met in the Army and started dating after boot camp. We had the same job, went to the same school and then got sent to different duty stations. He was in San Diego and I was in Norfolk. I guess we didn't really know each other. But I thought I was in love so when I got out, I moved here, to his home state."

Eve had pulled her chair from the backseat, attached the detachable wheels and transferred herself from the car. She remained focused on Abby, although she thought the woman found it easier to talk to someone who appeared to be distracted.

"How'd you find Mercy Ranch?" Eve asked after Abby suddenly went silent.

"I went to the VA yesterday. I thought I had a concussion. He beat my head against a door." Tears rolled down her cheeks and she removed the sunglasses to swipe them away. "I'm a strong, independent woman and I let a man beat me. I thought I could help him. The first couple of times he made excuses. I believed him."

"You're not a victim. You left."

She smiled at that. "Yeah, I guess I did. Anyway, I met Sierra there and she told me about Mercy Ranch. She called Jack for me."

"Mercy Ranch is a good place to start over."

"I'll stay for a little while. I can't go home to my parents. They'd never understand how he spent most of my money, beat me to the point of losing consciousness…"

"You're alive. That's the important thing," Eve said. And she realized how much truth there was in that statement. Not just for Abby, but for herself.

The church bell rang. Abby slipped her sunglasses back on. "I guess that's our cue."

"It is." Eve led the way to the church.

When they reached the ramp, Abby grabbed the handles of her chair. "Can I help?"

"Thanks."

They entered to find the usual crew from Mercy Ranch. They were all there, except Sierra and Ethan. She scanned the church, thinking he might have sat elsewhere. When she didn't see him, she took her spot at the end of a pew that had been shortened to make room for a wheelchair. Abby sat in the pew in front of her.

The music that morning was a blend of worship songs and old hymns. Eve closed her eyes, moved to tears by the songs in a way she hadn't experienced in a very long time. When the sermon started, she wasn't surprised that the message made her cry, as well . It was just the way the morning was going.

Of course the sermon would be about accepting the past in order to live in the present. She tried to close her mind to the words because she and God had been arguing for several years. She'd tried anger. She'd tried pleading. Nothing had changed her situation. This was her present and her future. Was she living in the present or lamenting the situation that had brought her here?

Pastor Jordan Stone was new. He wouldn't know her story or the times she'd left a service mid-sermon. He stood behind the pulpit, tall and very in command of the faith he preached. Of course, Sierra wouldn't want to work with him at the wedding chapel.

Church finally ended and she somehow felt lighter, freer than she had in months. As she left the church, Isaac's fiancée, Rebecca, joined her. She introduced herself to Abby as she tried to keep her daughter, Allie, from running off to join the other children.

"Do you know where Ethan is?" Eve asked Rebecca.

"I haven't seen him." She scanned the crowd and pointed at Allie. "Get back over here. Oh, wait a sec, I do know where he is."

Eve blinked a few times. "Am I supposed to keep up with this conversation?"

Rebecca dimpled at her remark. "You can try. Jack said that Tori caught the stomach bug. Ethan was up all night with her. He stayed home to take care of her."

Eve was surprised at the anger that washed over her. When Rebecca gave her a questioning look, she managed a smile.

"I'll have to check in on them."

Disappointment took the place of anger. Disappointment, hurt and several other emotions. He hadn't called her to help. Why? Because he thought she was the one who needed to be taken care of?

She'd show him who needed to be protected.

Ethan had moved himself and Tori to a small room at the back of Jack's log home, far from everyone. But he really didn't have much of a choice. The library, as Jack called it, had a desk, sleeper sofa, television and a wall of bookcases filled from top to bottom with books of every genre. One smaller bookcase near the desk contained Bibles, Bible studies, devotionals and self-help books. When he'd entered the room with Tori, he'd breathed in the scent of leather, polished wood and books.

He was so tired he no longer noticed how welcoming the room was, nor did he pay much attention to the windows that overlooked green fields and grazing cattle. Wind whipped at the trees and clouds covered the sun. He didn't care. Tori had finally fallen into an exhausted sleep after a night of battling the stomach virus. Fortunately Carson and Kylie West had made sure he was well equipped. He had bottles of water, snacks and grape popsicles for Tori.

No one had ever told him that being a parent could be this exhausting.

A knock on the door got him up off the sofa, where he'd managed to doze. Thirty minutes, he realized as he glanced at his watch.

He looked at Tori. She was still sleeping and crossed the room. He opened the door, and the person he found on the other side looked like she might be ready to do bodily harm.

He held a finger to his lips. She opened her mouth and closed it, her gaze shooting past him. He stepped into the hallway, closing the door so that it was open only a crack. Just in case Tori woke up.

"How is she?" Eve asked first. "And why didn't you tell me? You could have called me to tell me she was sick."

"I didn't think it was necessary to wake you up and make you come over in the middle of the night."

She tapped her fingers on the armrest of her chair and glared until he squirmed like a five-year-old caught eating candy before dinner. The problem was he'd done something wrong and didn't know what.

"I'm not sure why you thought I couldn't be counted on to help. We're supposed to be doing this together. *Together* means both of us."

"Oh, I get it. I wondered what I'd done to deserve this much anger."

She cocked her head the slightest bit to the side. "Do you get it?"

"I think so. I should have called you, and I'm sorry. Now you think that I think you're not capable. Everything I do is measured to the horse I thought you couldn't handle."

Her chin came up a notch, much like the teenager he'd once known. He bit back a smile because he guessed that wasn't the best response to her ire.

"I'm sorry, Eve," he started. "I really do know that you're capable. I left her with you that first day. And then for two days after that. I obviously know you can

Get Up To 4 Free Books!

Dear Reader,

IT'S A FACT: if you answer 4 quick questions, we'll send you 4 FREE REWARDS from each series you try!

Try **Love Inspired® Romance Larger-Print** books featuring Christian characters facing modern-day challenges.

Try **Love Inspired® Suspense Larger-Print** novels featuring Christian characters facing challenges to their faith... and lives

Or **TRY BOTH!**

I'm not kidding you. As a leading publisher of women's fiction, we value your opinions... and your time. That's why we are prepared to reward you handsomely for completing our mini-survey. In fact, we have 4 Free Rewards for you, including 2 free books and 2 free gifts from each series you try!

Thank you for participating in our survey,

Pam Powers

To get your 4 FREE REWARDS:

Complete the survey below and return the insert today to receive up to 4 FREE BOOKS and FREE GIFTS guaranteed!

"4 for 4" MINI-SURVEY

1 Is reading one of your favorite hobbies?
☐ YES ☐ NO

2 Do you prefer to read instead of watch TV?
☐ YES ☐ NO

3 Do you read newspapers and magazines?
☐ YES ☐ NO

4 Do you enjoy trying new book series with FREE BOOKS?
☐ YES ☐ NO

Please send me my Free Rewards, consisting of **2 Free Books from each series I select** and **Free Mystery Gifts**. I understand that I am under no obligation to buy anything, as explained on the back of this card.

❏ **Love Inspired® Romance Larger-Print** (122/322 IDL GNPV)
❏ **Love Inspired® Suspense Larger-Print** (107/307 IDL GNPV)
❏ **Try Both** (122/322/107/307 IDL GNP7)

FIRST NAME   LAST NAME

ADDRESS

APT.#   CITY

STATE/PROV.   ZIP/POSTAL CODE

READER SERVICE—Here's how it works:

Accepting your 2 free books and 2 free gifts (gifts valued at approximately $10.00 retail) places you under no obligation to buy anything. You may keep the books and gifts and return the shipping statement marked "cancel." If you do not cancel, approximately one month later we'll send you 6 more books from each series you have chosen, and bill you at our low, subscribers-only discount price. Love Inspired® Romance Larger-Print books and Love Inspired® Suspense Larger-Print books consist of 6 books each month and cost just $5.74 each in the U.S. or $6.24 each in Canada. That is a savings of at least 18% off the cover price. It's quite a bargain! Shipping and handling is just 50¢ per book in the U.S. and 75¢ per book in Canada*. You may return any shipment at our expense and cancel at any time — or you may continue to receive monthly shipments at our low, subscribers-only discount price plus shipping and handling. *Terms and prices subject to change without notice. Prices do not include sales taxes which will be charged (if applicable) based on your state or country of residence. Canadian residents will be charged applicable taxes. Offer not valid in Quebec. Books received may not be as shown. All orders subject to approval. Credit or debit balances in a customer's account(s) may be offset by any other outstanding balance owed by or to the customer. Please allow 3 to 4 weeks for delivery. Offer available while quantities last.

▲ If offer card is missing write to: Reader Service, P.O. Box 1341, Buffalo, NY 14240-8531 or visit www.ReaderService.com ▲

BUSINESS REPLY MAIL

FIRST-CLASS MAIL   PERMIT NO. 717   BUFFALO, NY

POSTAGE WILL BE PAID BY ADDRESSEE

READER SERVICE
PO BOX 1341
BUFFALO NY 14240-8571

NO POSTAGE
NECESSARY
IF MAILED
IN THE
UNITED STATES

handle caring for her. She was sick and I didn't really think about calling and waking you up."

"Next time you will," she insisted.

"Next time I will."

"May I come in?"

He pushed the door open. She zoomed in ahead of him and went straight to the playpen. She peered over the side at the sleeping child, her expression softening. Ethan stopped next to her, his hand resting on her shoulder. She stiffened beneath his touch but then she covered his hand with her own.

"I'm so sad that Hanna and James will miss out on seeing her grow up. I'm so sad that she won't know them." Her voice broke and she swiped at tears running down her cheeks.

"I know."

"I do not understand life. I don't understand why some are taken and others…"

She didn't finish her thought. Backing away from him, she turned to look out the window. He didn't follow. He knew when she needed space. Experience had taught him that much.

After several minutes of silence, she moved to face him with more sadness than he'd ever expected to see in anyone's eyes.

"I can live with what happened to me. I can't live with knowing that somehow our coordinates were manipulated by an enemy we couldn't see and suddenly we were in an isolated area, nowhere near our destination. I was the person in charge of navigation. I was the one responsible."

He remained silent, knowing she didn't need to hear that he was sorry.

"Two of my men died that day. Because of me."

"Not because of you. Because an unseen enemy changed your coordinates."

She closed her eyes. "I tell myself that. Every day I wake up telling myself it's okay to be alive. That God is in control. But it doesn't change the fact that they died and I'm still alive."

He ran a hand through his hair, unsure of his next move. "Can we sit together? On the sofa?"

A hint of a smile tugged at her lips. "Yes, we can sit together. And no, I don't need your help."

"That's too bad, because I like helping. Actually, I felt strong and heroic when I picked you up the other day."

"Don't make me feel like an invalid."

"If I ever do anything to make you feel that way, tell me?"

She held out a hand. "Deal."

He took her hand in his, then couldn't let go. He lifted her hand to his lips. "Deal."

"Oh, no you don't." She pulled her hand from his. "Please don't."

She moved her chair parallel to the sofa and shifted, moving her feet to the floor and then bracing her hand on the sofa to transfer herself. Once she was seated, she patted the sofa next to her and Ethan sat down. The two feet of space between them seemed necessary. For her peace of mind. For his sanity.

"And we know that all things work together for good to them that love God." She spoke the words of the verse, then sighed. "That's the verse I try to remember. God didn't create sin and suffering. All things mean good things and bad things work together for good. Right?"

"Right. I wish it was as easy as reminding myself of that verse. It isn't. When I think about Hanna and James being gone, and raising their daughter… I don't want to raise her alone, Eve."

"I know." Her attention focused on the sleeping child in the playpen. Briefly she closed her eyes. "I know. And I say the verse because Kylie told me to, but that doesn't mean I'm not angry or that I've figured out how to connect my faith with the tragedies that happen all around me."

"Tori isn't a tragedy, she's a tiny person depending on us."

"I don't mean that *she's* the tragedy. She is perfect and sweet and deserves every good thing. I just don't know if I can be her mother. Oh, wow, that word." She gasped. *"Father. Mother.* We have to step up, be her parents. But the two of us, we're not married. We can't give her a whole family, can we?"

"We can figure it out together," he offered. But he knew that his heart was on the line and maybe hers was off-limits.

The person sitting next to him was not the girl he'd grown up with, the woman he'd planned to marry. Life and circumstances had changed her, had changed them both. Whatever he'd thought before, he now knew there was no going back.

They had to discover each other as if they were strangers. Only then could they truly move forward.

Chapter Nine

Eve realized she'd been so busy fighting this guardianship, she hadn't thought about Tori as a little toddler calling for her mommy. Who would that mommy be? The ramifications of that reality were stunning. As she sat there watching the little girl sleep, she thought about a future with Tori in her life, needing hugs, needing attention. Needing parents.

The past four years had taught Eve a lot about her strengths and weaknesses. In one day that went horribly wrong, everything had changed. But wasn't that how tragedy happened? A person was never expecting it. There was nothing safe or certain in life. Trust was the safety net. Faith that all things, even the bad, could work together for good was the belief that held it all together. Even when Eve doubted. Even when she was angry.

Her circumstances no longer made her angry. She'd made peace with her paralysis. She knew her abilities and focused on those rather than on her disabilities. She found that other people had to be taught to do the same, to focus on what she could do rather than what she couldn't.

But in the beginning she'd been filled with so many doubts, so many fears. And the biggest fear had been not really what she couldn't do, but losing herself. Losing herself to the well-meaning people in her life, the ones who wanted to take care of her, fix things for her, make sure she was safe.

She'd needed independence. And so she'd pushed away the people who loved her. Including the man sitting next to her. She regretted so many things but she knew she couldn't go back. She knew it because when Tori was sick, he hadn't called her. He'd confirmed what she feared, that he thought of her as a disabled person, not a person with abilities.

"You okay?" he asked.

She drew in a deep breath and smiled. Because telling him how she felt was pointless. He'd argue, and she'd still feel the same way.

"I'm good. I'm worried about her. She's so still."

"She had a long night."

"I know. Do you think she's over the worst of it?"

"Time will tell."

"Have you eaten?" she asked.

"Breakfast." He leaned back on the couch and stretched his legs out. "I'm trying to avoid the main part of the house. I don't want this to spread even more than it already has."

"I think it's inevitable," she told him. "It's a stomach virus. They don't seem to like to stay contained."

"No, they don't. I'm just sorry I brought it with me."

"It's a virus, not the plague."

He laughed, and she thought about how that laugh always made her feel better. It still did.

They had so many shared memories. She'd forced herself to let go of those memories, since it had made things easier for her. But she realized that she'd missed him. Ethan and his family had been the most normal part of her childhood. Not that she'd had a horrible childhood, or that her parents hadn't loved her. They did love her.

The door opened slightly and Maria quietly said, *"Hola."*

"Come in." Ethan got up to greet her. "You must be feeling better."

"Much better!" Maria's eyes widened when she saw Eve. "Oh, Evie, we don't want you to get this virus."

Eve brushed off the concern. "I'll be fine."

"I hope so. This isn't a fun virus. I can tell you from personal experience, unfortunately." Maria pushed a cart of food into the room. "I have sandwiches, salad, fruit and cookies. Eve, I'll go back and get more. You need to eat."

"I'm fine, Maria. You don't have to do that."

"I want to. You're too skinny."

Eve shook her head at that. "I'm healthy."

"Yes, you're healthy. But too skinny. You take it from me, you need to eat. I'll bring more food."

"I love you, Maria."

"I love you, too, Evie. How's that baby girl doing? Did you give her that ginger tea in her bottle?"

Ethan held up a bottle with amber-colored liquid inside. "She drank a little before she fell asleep."

"The ginger will settle her tummy," Maria said. "Okay, you two eat. I'll be back with more food."

Eve didn't bother to argue. She knew Maria loved to feed people more than she loved almost anything else. Except maybe Jack West, whom she doted on with unabashed affection.

The door closed and, almost as if on cue, Tori began to cry. Ethan leaned over the playpen and picked her up, and as he did she lost the contents of her stomach all over his shirt. Then she started to wail.

"Give her to me," Eve said. "You're going to have to change."

"I don't know, Eve."

"I know. You didn't call me when she was sick, you don't think you can leave her with me, but you want me to take my place as guardian?" She reached for the baby. "Give her to me. Now."

He still hesitated so she gave him a warning look. He handed over the baby.

"I'll go change. There are diapers and wipes in the bag next to the playpen." He reached into the bag for the container of wipes and pulled one out to dab at his hands and shirt. "I'll only be gone a few minutes."

"And I'm sure Tori and I will be just fine while you're gone."

"Eve," he started. She raised a hand to stop the apology that was sure to follow. "I'll be back."

He left the room, and she looked at the miserable little girl in her arms.

"Someday you'll be a teenager and he's going to worry about you. He'll pack your first car in Bubble Wrap, try to make you run barrels on a stick horse, because he won't want you to get thrown. You'll have to stand your ground and let him know that you can have a real horse. I might not be living with you, but I'll always be here to help you. I'll teach you to stand your ground." She paused at that. "But he has the best intentions for you. He's going to be a good dad."

For some silly reason, her vision suddenly got cloudy and a tear trickled down her cheek. She hadn't cried this much since the days right after the accident.

"Let's get you changed." She then realized her poor planning. Still on the couch, the diaper bag a good ten feet away, a crying baby in her arms. "Okay, we need a plan, little miss."

She pulled the blanket off the back of the sofa and placed Tori on it, then she used throw pillows to cocoon the baby and keep her from rolling too close to the edge. Eve brushed a hand over the tiny head and Tori smiled.

"Okay, stay put."

Eve transferred herself to her chair. She hooked the diaper bag over the handles, grabbed the bottle of ginger tea and, on her way past the cart, took one of the sandwiches meant for Ethan. On second thought, she also grabbed a cookie.

Tori started to fuss. Eve reached to pick her up and the baby vomited again. Eve cringed as she held the child away from her. The wood floors could be cleaned. The idea of cleaning her chair was not so pleasant.

After a full minute, Eve cradled the now exhausted Tori against her chest. They both smelled. They were both messy. And the sandwich had fallen on the floor. It didn't matter. She leaned back, cradling the sick little girl.

"We have to get you changed," she whispered. "I have a feeling you won't be happy about this. But it's gotta be done."

She moved to the sofa, where she placed Tori on the seat. She decided it would be easier to do this if she was next to her, so she transferred herself to the sofa. Once situated, she grabbed the bag and she was able to get Tori cleaned up with wipes and changed.

"You need a bath," she informed the little girl.

Tori didn't seem to care. She nestled in close and fell asleep. Eve eyed the sandwich on the floor. Her stomach rumbled and she acknowledged that the sandwich would have been good.

Just then the door opened. Ethan entered, his hair damp, his shirt clean.

"You took a shower," she accused.

"I didn't mean to be gone so long but it required more than just a change of clothes." He glanced around the room. "Something happen while I was gone?"

"I decided to change her clothes, which required the bag, and that required I go right past that tray of food. Unfortunately she started to get sick again." She pointed to the floor. "You'll have to clean that up."

He grimaced. "That isn't pleasant."

"I've been told that being a parent is a blessing." She smirked.

"Yeah, I've been told the same. No one mentions moments like this."

"Nope. I think it's much worse than housebreaking a puppy."

"Agreed. I'll run down to the kitchen to see about

paper towels and some kind of cleaner. You'll…" He stopped himself.

"It's fine. Go."

He left, the door closing softly behind him. Eve relaxed against the back of the sofa, Tori snug in her arms. In her sleep the little girl sobbed, her body shuddering. Eve stroked her arm the way she'd seen Kylie do with her children. She sang "Jesus Loves Me." After a few minutes, Tori's mouth went slack as she slipped into a sound sleep.

"Sweet baby," Eve whispered.

Her own eyes grew heavy. She pulled the throw pillow close and rested her arm on it. In her sleep, Tori snuggled in closer. Eve wondered what the child knew. Did she have the ability to wonder where her parents had gone to, or was it a more abstract missing of someone and knowing they were absent from her life?

But the thoughts were too much. She had to focus on Tori, on making her life happier. She realized that in one week she'd gone from wanting to push Ethan and Tori away to wondering how she could remain a part of this child's life. At least in some small way, she wanted to be included.

Or maybe she wanted more than a tiny corner of Tori's life. But that life included Ethan. And Ethan was a detriment to her independence.

She sighed as her thoughts grew muddled and decided it was easier to just take an afternoon nap as the rain pattered against the roof.

Maria smiled up at him when he entered the kitchen. "Ethan, can I get you something?" she asked.

"I'm afraid so. Cleaning supplies. Tori got sick."

"Oh no! That poor baby girl." She wiped her hands on a towel. "We keep those in the pantry. But I will clean that as soon as I finish up here."

"There's no need for you to do that. Just point the way."

"Down the hall and to the left."

He followed her directions and when he returned to the kitchen, Maria and the tray of food were gone but Kylie and Carson West had arrived with their two children, as well as the baby they were fostering.

"How's Tori?" Carson asked as he headed for the fridge. "Is there tea in here?"

"I didn't look for tea," Ethan answered. "And Tori seems a little better. Maria made her some ginger tea."

"Maria knows best." Carson pulled a pitcher of iced tea from the fridge. "And she never fails to keep tea. Do you want a glass?"

"No, I should get back to the girls."

"You mean Tori and Eve?" Kylie asked. Still holding baby Cara, she sat down on one of the bar stools.

"Yes, that's who I mean." Was he in trouble?

"Can I give you some advice, Ethan?" Kylie asked. He kind of thought he didn't have a choice.

Carson cleared his throat and shot Ethan a warning look. "Say yes because she's going to give it anyway. And she's usually right."

Kylie West smiled at her husband. "That's why I love you. You're so smart."

"I'll take that advice," Ethan said.

"Don't let Eve's wheelchair fool you into thinking she's an invalid or that she needs you to take care of her. She can do almost anything, and if she can't, she'll ask for help."

"I appreciate the advice." He knew that about Eve, that she could do anything she set her mind to. She'd always been that way. Maybe the problem was he wanted to take care of her, to protect her.

"She's my best friend," Kylie said, obviously a warning.

"I know. She was my best friend, too." He left because he didn't know what else to say.

A moment later he peeked through the door to see how Tori and Eve were faring. They were both asleep. He slipped quietly into the room, careful not to wake them. The sight of Eve and Tori undid something inside him, filling him with a mixture of regret and hope. And the sense of being whole for the first time in four years. No, six. He hadn't been whole since she'd left for the duty station that would eventually take her to Afghanistan.

He'd tried to convince himself that the emptiness inside him would close up, the way a wound closes, leaving scars but being basically healed. It hadn't happened. She'd been too much a part of his heart, too much a part of his life for too many years.

But the woman sitting on the couch with Tori was a different woman from the one he'd planned to marry. She needed something different from him. Or maybe she was the same woman and she was only just now making it clear that she needed something different, something she'd needed the entire time they'd dated.

He would have to figure out if he could be the man she wanted or needed. He'd have to figure out if she even wanted him in her life. But it wasn't all about him. Maybe he wasn't the man she wanted or needed?

For now he had to concentrate on Tori. He had to focus on how to secure her future, how to give her the stability and love a child deserved.

Quietly he went to work cleaning up the mess. Eve and Tori slept on, even after he left the room to toss the trash. He came back in and disinfected the floor; although he'd cleaned it, Maria said to disinfect, disinfect, disinfect.

When he stood, she was watching him, her dark eyes amused.

"What? I can clean."

"Yes, you can. I'm impressed. I'll admit, getting down on the floor and scrubbing was not on my to-do list." She smiled. "There are things I admit I can't do. I could clean that floor but it requires a lot of effort and energy. I work out, but with specialized equipment. I can't go riding, which is obvious."

He started to disagree with that, but she felt it was the truth so he refrained. "But you've found more things you can do than things you can't."

"True. When I first woke up in the hospital and couldn't move, that was the most frightened I've ever been in my life. I was in a dark place, thinking of how my life had changed and of all the things I'd never do again. Climb a mountain, ride a horse, go for a run. Dance with you."

"I can't imagine your fear."

"I worked through them. I focused on my strengths."

He wanted to tell her she was amazing but he had a feeling she didn't want to hear it. She didn't see herself as amazing. She saw herself the way any woman would, as a person just living her life. Obstacles, challenges, victories, doubts. They were all a part of life.

But to him, she would always be amazing.

She scooted to the edge of the sofa and transferred back to her chair. Tori grew restless and Eve moved into position, picking the baby up and holding her on her lap. With her free hand, she backed up, facing him.

"She feels warm again. Do you have the medicine for her fever?"

He picked up the bottle he'd left on the desk. "Carson said to give her a half dropper of this. I didn't get much in her earlier, and then she lost what little she did take when she got sick."

"Let's try again."

"Carson and Kylie are here," he offered. "Should I go get them?"

"Because we can't manage to give a tiny little baby a dropper of medicine? Come on, where's your spirit of adventure?"

He laughed at that. "It's in the clothes hamper with my shirt."

"I'll hold her, you get the medicine ready." Eve gave him a look that challenged. "Come on, you can do it."

"Let me wash my hands and toss these paper towels."

"Good idea."

He returned and she watched as he filled the dropper, then squirted half the liquid back into the bottle. Tori whimpered and cried a little.

"She's half asleep," Ethan said. "I'm afraid we'll end up wearing this stuff."

"I have a technique with the puppies that might work," she suggested with a grin.

"What do I need to do?"

"I'll hold her. Squirt the medicine into the side of her

cheek. I'm not sure why that works but it does. And not so fast that she chokes or that it makes her sick."

She did her part, holding Tori gently but firmly. He got the medicine dropper into her mouth and gently squeezed. She cried and fought, but most of the liquid seemed to stay inside.

"You're a natural at this," he complimented. Her eyes widened and she shook her head a little.

"No, I'm not a natural. And I'm not prepared for this."

"Neither of us were prepared. That doesn't mean we can't have some skills. Look, I don't want to always be saying the wrong thing to you so let's have a real conversation where you tell me what is okay and what isn't. If I know your expectations, maybe I can get this right."

She exhaled and seemed to deflate, her gaze lowering to watch Tori. The baby had fallen back to sleep and cuddled against her.

"I apologize. When you say it like that, I sound like a shrew. I don't mean to be defensive, it's just that I've fought so hard to get where I am."

"I'm listening," he said.

"Okay, first and foremost, I'm happy with my life. It's taken several years for me to be able to say that."

That was where he had to tread carefully, because she'd been here, content and living a life she'd chosen for herself, and he'd been left behind wondering why she'd walked away.

"My turn," he said.

"Okay."

"I'm not sure how to process that we were going to get married but you were able to walk away and rebuild your life without regretting the loss of us."

Her expression softened. "That isn't what I meant. I did miss you. I missed us. And I'm so sorry for what I did. I can't take it back but I'm sorry. At the same time I needed to be here so I can't regret that."

"I get that."

"I'm comfortable here, Ethan. At this ranch, in my apartment, in this chair. The chair is my freedom, it's my legs. It's not a detriment to my life, it gives me independence. Where would I be without it? I'd be stuck on that couch, in my bed, unable to drive or go places I want to go. Stop seeing me as this chair."

He moved a club chair away from the window and positioned it in front of her. "What do you need from me?"

"I need for you to trust that I can take care of myself. That I can even take care of other people."

"I'm going to do my best to respect that. You know that my wanting to take care of you didn't start the day I saw you in this wheelchair."

"I know that, Ethan. That's why I ended our relationship. I wanted to be your partner in life. What I've learned is, I don't want to be anyone's responsibility. I don't want to be in a relationship with someone who doesn't know me or understand what I need."

She wanted freedom. And he still wanted their dream. The horse ranch, the children, growing old together with grandchildren playing in the backyard.

That their dreams had taken different directions seemed to be an obstacle. But the very fact that she was sitting and having this conversation with him gave him hope.

And hope was a place to start.

Chapter Ten

Eve closed her laptop and leaned back, stretching her arms above her head. And dropped her pen. She leaned over to pick it up but it had rolled too far. Fortunately she had a visitor. Tex, the chocolate Labradoodle that normally spent his day with Joe, was sprawled out on the floor next to her. She snapped her fingers and the dog sat up. His ears perked and he watched the pen roll away from her chair.

"I can get that." Glory jumped up from the floor where she'd been playing with Tori.

"No, that's okay." Eve held up a hand to stop the teen from moving. "Let Tex, it's his job."

"Oh, that's right. I forgot about him. He was like a big area rug until he moved."

"He's hairier than any area rug." She looked at the big Lab with fondness. He was just a puppy but he had a lot of potential as a service dog.

She gave a command for him to retrieve and the Labrador stopped midstretch and went after the pen. An ink pen was much harder for his big mouth to handle than, say, a stick, but he managed. He used a paw to stop the pen from moving and gently lifted it in his mouth. He brought it to her, gently dropping it in her hand.

"I'd like to learn to do that," Glory said, clearly in awe of the dog. She laughed. "I mean, I don't want to learn to fetch. I'd like to learn to train these dogs. Could I take one of the pups home with me and work with him? Kylie said you farm the puppies out when they're a few months old. People take them and socialize them until they're ready for serious training."

"I think that might be a possibility. The puppies I have now won't go to a home for another six weeks or so." That reminded her. "We never talked about your aptitude test."

"I thought maybe I failed. I mean, I didn't do very well in school."

"Actually, you did really well on the test. Tell me what you'd like to do with your life, Glory."

The teenager smiled shyly at the baby on the colorful mat. Tori played with her toes for a moment and then she rolled to her tummy and reached for a rattle that she shoved in her mouth. She'd recovered from the stomach virus but didn't really seem to be back to her normal self. Carson had told her not to worry, yet. But she did.

Glory pushed a fall of blond hair back from her face. "I'd like to be a teacher. I mean, I know I'm the last person anyone would want teaching their children but I'd like to teach. Especially smaller kids."

"There's no reason you couldn't or shouldn't be a teacher, Glory. I think you'd be excellent."

"Thank you," she said, her cheeks turning a little

bit pink. "But I don't know the first thing about doing something like that."

"We can help you, Glory."

The girl shook her head, swiping a tear from the corner of her eye. "I can't even tell you how much that would mean to me."

Eve backed away from her desk. "It would mean a lot to me if I could help you. Would you like to walk out to the stable with me?"

As much as she liked to avoid the stable, there were times she just couldn't.

"Of course." Glory pushed to her feet. "Do you want me to carry Tori or do you want her on your lap?"

"We'll put her on my lap if you don't mind getting the baby sling."

"Okay." Glory lifted Tori, kissed her on the cheek and set her on Eve's lap. Then reached over to the table to get the sling, all smiles. "I know this is a crazy thing to say, Miss Eve, but losing Cara might have been the best thing to ever happen to me. It brought you all into my life. And it got me back in church. Who knew something that hard could turn out to be a blessing?"

Eve brushed a kiss across the top of Tori's head to hide the emotion that welled up inside her. "God brings us blessings, Glory, sometimes in the hardest, most heartbreaking ways."

All things work together for good... Even the most difficult.

Eve closed her eyes and drew in a deep breath as the verse touched her mind and heart. Some things were so stinking hard and so good, all at the same time. And it didn't seem right, to find a blessing like Tori at the expense of such tragedy.

She cleared her throat and managed a bright smile for the teenager watching her with concern in her blue eyes.

"Let's go to the stable." She said it as cheerfully as possible.

"I'm sorry if I upset you."

"Oh, Glory, you didn't. You actually made my day. You reminded me of something important. You reminded me that out of ashes God can build beauty."

Glory hugged her tight, encompassing Tori in the embrace. "Okay, let's go to the stable."

They were a short distance from the stable when she saw a truck and trailer pull in to the front entrance of Mercy Ranch. Isaac and his new horse. Rebecca had texted, telling her she had to see this animal of Isaac's. It wasn't often that Rebecca texted and even more curious that she wanted Eve to see a horse. As if there weren't a good thirty head of horses on the ranch already.

"That's a pretty fancy trailer," Glory said from behind the chair. She'd taken the handles and was pushing Eve across the rougher patches of ground.

"It is a nice trailer." She guessed the trailer could haul four horses and had living quarters.

As they got closer she was surprised to see Ethan's truck parked near the barn. The door opened and he jumped out. He'd been in Tulsa since the previous day, leaving only after he was sure that Tori was over the worst of her stomach virus. They'd spent two days taking turns holding the baby, cleaning up after her and sleeping when they could.

Ethan waved but then he headed for the trailer that

Isaac backed up to the stable. A few of the other hands came out to see what Isaac had brought home.

"That's a lot of commotion for a horse," Glory said.

"Yeah, I'm guessing this isn't just any horse. Isaac bought him from a ranch in Arizona. He's supposed to be one of the best cutting horses in the country."

Glory whistled. "That's impressive. And I don't even know what a cutting horse is."

"I'm sure after they get him settled you'll get to watch. Basically there is a small herd of steers and heifers that are kept in a group by other riders. The cutting horse and his rider will cut a calf from the herd and keep him separated from the group."

"Oh, I see. We didn't go to rodeos much when I was a kid." Glory laughed at that. "Actually we didn't do much of anything. My parents never had money and if they did, they spent it on drugs."

"Glory, once you get Cara back, you're going to be a good mom. You're going to give her—and yourself—a completely different life from the one you led as a child."

"I hope so. I really want that."

"I know you do."

Isaac opened the back of the trailer and a moment later led the dark bay stallion down the ramp. The horse was a deep red with a black mane and tail, black stockinged legs and a white stripe down his face. He pranced around the stable yard as if he knew just how beautiful he was.

Tori clapped and gurgled a few unintelligible sounds. All of six months and she already loved horses. Eve gave her a quick hug and kissed her cheeks, which left the little girl giggling.

Eve stopped when she saw that Ethan had stepped

inside the trailer. Isaac led the stallion into the stable, stroking the horse's neck as he went. But he stopped being the focus of Eve's attention. Her gaze traveled to the trailer where she could still hear hooves stomping. A high pitched whinny vibrated from the interior.

Ethan exited the trailer, leading a pretty gray gelding out. The horse had the head of an Arabian, as well as the shorter back and higher tail carriage. As his hooves touched the ground, the animal stopped, ears perked, as he surveyed his surroundings.

"Glory, can you take the baby?"

"Of course I can." Glory walked around to the front of Eve's chair.

Eve undid the sling and held the baby up to the teenager. "Thank you."

She pushed herself closer to the horse. Ethan pretended he didn't notice. He took a saddle out of the trailer and, as Eve watched, he put the tack on the animal. She guessed the horse to be around fifteen hands. A nice size for an Arab.

"What do you think?" Ethan asked as he finished cinching up the saddle.

"He's nice. An Arabian. I didn't think you were a fan of the hot-blooded breeds. Isn't that what you told my dad?"

"I might have been wrong. I've been rethinking a lot of things lately."

She bit back a smile. "Have you really? And why is that?"

"As much as I like to think I'm always right, there is a possibility, slim but still there, that I can be wrong."

"But not often?"

"Definitely not often." He slid a hand down the horse's sleek gray neck. "This guy, for instance. I am not wrong in thinking he is a decent horse. He rides double. He can go all day long."

"Because Arabians are endurance animals."

"Yes," he said. "A friend once told me that but I thought hot-blooded horses couldn't be trusted. And they could never be barrel horses."

"I'm impressed with your humility."

He winked and put his left foot in the stirrup. The horse shifted, then turned with the slightest shift of the reins. "He's very responsive. He's ten years old and has been ridden on trail rides, and also used in endurance competition. The young woman who owned him said she was just trading him for a younger horse. Otherwise she would have kept him."

"That's all very interesting. And where's Rebecca? She texted and told me to come down here."

Ethan swung off the horse and landed next to her. She put her hand out, wondering if the horse would shy away from her chair. He didn't. Instead he extended his head to allow her to pet him on the jaw.

"Oh, she texted you for me." He swung around to where Glory stood. "Could you take Tori up to the house? Kylie is there and she said the two of you could handle her."

"Of course we can," Glory responded. An amused look shifted her features and she gave Eve a knowing look. "You have fun, Miss Eve."

"I'll be up in a few minutes, Glory."

"No, you won't." Ethan leaned. "Grab hold."

"What?"

He pointed to his neck. "I said grab hold."

She put her arms around his neck and he lifted her from her chair. Before she could protest, he put her on the horse. And then he swung up behind her.

"What are you doing?" She shifted to look back at him. "Ethan, I can't do this. I can't ride a horse. I can't feel. I can't hold on with my legs."

"I'm here, right behind you. I'm putting your feet in the stirrups." True to his word, he leaned, putting first her left and then her right foot in the stirrups. She watched, not feeling his hand on her feet. "Now, relax against me. I've got this."

"What if he bucks? What if something happens?"

"I wouldn't do this if I wasn't completely comfortable with this horse. I rode him for five hours yesterday. I took him through water, by the highway, in and out of barns, through gates. I'm confident we're safe or you wouldn't be up here with me. But you love horses. You love to ride. And you should. Because paraplegics ride horses, too."

She shook her head, not wanting to argue with him but also not able to get the words out because the emotions were thick, making it difficult to say anything.

His arms went around her and he put the reins in her hands.

"I'm right here," he spoke, his breath warm against her cheek.

She sat silently, trying to orient herself to the idea of being in a saddle and not feeling the saddle, not feeling the horse. She needed to be grounded. She touched the horse with her hands, calming herself as she did.

"You're in charge," he spoke quietly from behind

her. "I'm here to catch you, to keep you safe, but this is your moment."

"My moment." She gave a shaky laugh. "I'm upset with you."

The horse obeyed the slightest touch of the rein against his neck. She headed him in the direction of the trail through the back hayfield, an unfenced section used for trail rides. Rides she'd never participated in. How could she? Someone would have to lift her on and off a horse. She'd have to trust the horse because what if she needed to get down? What if the horse spooked? All of the fears teased her, taking her confidence even with Ethan behind her.

"Why are you upset with me?" Ethan asked as they rode in the shade of a line of trees.

"Because you can't make decisions for me the way you used to."

"Okay, I apologize."

"I'm serious, Ethan. I do not like having control taken away. You think you can pick me up, move me where you want me. I don't want to be manipulated or handled." The more she talked, the more upset she got. The horse's ears pricked, moving to pick up her voice.

"I'm sorry." Ethan's hand brushed down her arm and she shivered beneath the touch that was too much.

"Imagine if I forced you to go where I wanted when I wanted? You picked me up and put me in this saddle without even asking if I wanted to be here. The moment you took me out of my chair, you took away my power."

"I'm so sorry," his voice rasped. "Forgive me, Eve."

"It's the barrel horse all over again. You chose for me."

"I get it. I wanted to do something for you, something

amazing. And what I did was take control. I'm learning but it might take me a while to get it."

"I know. And I'm going to have to work on not being so easily upset by your little surprises." She sighed. "He is nice."

They continued to ride in silence. Peace stole over her. She felt a calm she hadn't felt in a long time. The air along the tree line was shady and cool. Other than the sound of the horse's hooves on the dry ground, and a few birds flitting from tree to tree, there was silence.

She felt Ethan starting to say something. She shook her head.

He remained silent. Eve closed her eyes, knowing he was there, a safety net. The rhythm of the horse rocked her, and if she kept her eyes closed she could almost believe she could feel the animal, almost believe it was her legs carrying her. She drew in a breath and felt Ethan's hand tighten on her arm, giving a light squeeze.

"I missed this. So much," she admitted with some chagrin. "I'm so mad at you, so how can I be so happy that you did this?"

"Those dialectics, who understands how we can feel both at the same time? I've felt the same in the past ten days. I'm glad to be here in this moment with you. I'm also angry that I've missed four years of moments like this."

"But you understand."

"I understand."

The horse perked up, obviously smelling the water from the creek. Eve guided him to an area that she knew from riding in the truck to this location. She brought him to an easy stop in a small glade where once they'd seen a deer and twin fawns during an early morning drive. Today a fox ran across the clearing. The horse raised his head to watch, his ears following the path of the canine-like twin antennae.

"We could sit here for a while?" Ethan suggested.

Sit for a while. She liked the idea even if it meant being handled by him. There were moments when a person had to let go of their pride.

Ethan steadied Eve, then he swung down, landing next to the horse. As expected, Twister stood without moving.

"Now, how do you plan to get me down from here?" Eve taunted.

He went to the off side of the horse and moved her right foot from the stirrup. Then he moved back to the left side of the horse and extracted that sneakered foot. "Hands on my shoulders and I'll…"

"Wait, give me a moment. I'll move my leg over if you'll hold him steady. Does he have a name?"

"Twister. As in Texas Twister."

"Poor boy, just because he's gray he's named after weather. Okay, let me do this."

She lifted her right leg, leaned back and then moved it to the near side of the horse, turning her body slightly toward him. "Now I'll put my hands on your shoulders."

"And I'll lift you down."

"Don't drop me."

He smiled up at her. "I would never drop you."

Her hands settled on his shoulders and he paused to look up, meeting her gaze, which held no uncertainty. He put one arm under her knees and as she leaned in, locking her arms behind his neck, he eased her from the saddle. It was awkward but it worked, and the end result was Eve in his arms.

"Can you grab the reins and lead him?" he asked. "We'll sit over here where we can see the creek."

"Mmm-hmm," was her response.

Gently he set her down on the ground. She positioned her legs in front of her and braced herself on her arms to look up at the canopy of trees that protected them from the early afternoon sun.

"It's warm," he said as he dropped down next to her.

"Yes, it's May. It's always warm in May."

He laughed. "Okay, I didn't know what else to say."

"Thank you for taking me riding."

"You're welcome. He's yours. My gift to you."

She shook her head. "Why would you do that?"

"Because you love to ride. You should have a horse you can enjoy."

"How did you find him?" she asked, looking up at the animal that loomed over her. "Do you think you could tie him? This is unnerving."

"Agreed." He got up and led the horse to a nearby post that was obviously meant for tying horses.

She watched him the entire time. When he returned to her side, she looked up at him. "So…about the horse?"

"I saw him advertised online. His rider was a woman, a paraplegic. She used him in different events, mostly endurance, some trail classes."

"Ethan, you shouldn't have."

"But I did. You can decide if you want to keep him, sell him or give him away."

"My decision to make. Thank you." She leaned her

head against his shoulder and he moved his left arm behind her to brace her.

"Yes, your decision."

"We have a lot of those coming up." She closed her eyes, relaxing next to him. "I really am praying about this. I don't want to do the wrong thing for the right reasons, or vice versa."

"I know."

"Speaking of hard decisions to make, I'm thinking about talking to my parents. I mean, more than talking. I need to be honest with them. About everything."

"I'm glad to hear that. I think talking to them is an important step for your future."

They sat quietly for some time. When she looked up, questions in her dark eyes, he touched his lips to hers. Her hand moved to his cheek, holding him. As if he would ever try to escape. She was the woman he'd planned to spend his life with.

She sighed. Her eyes were closed so he kissed her eyelids. A smile tipped her mouth. He kissed the corners of her lips.

"Stop." She spoke softly, putting some distance between them. "We have to stop because this just confuses the issue. When you kiss me, I think we're still the same people we were, but we aren't."

"Agreed. We are not the same people."

"We have to think about Tori."

"Again, I agree."

She scooted away from him. "You stay over there, I'll stay here."

He almost smiled. "Okay. We have four weeks to

come up with a plan for Tori. Our court date is at the middle of June."

"Prepare what? I mean, we go before a judge. What do we prepare?"

"A plan for guardianship. He wants to see two parents ready and willing to raise her as their own, provide a home, love and support for her."

"I just can't imagine what that judge is going to say when we enter his courtroom to tell him we—in all of our dysfunction—are the people James and Hanna chose to raise their daughter."

"We have to show a united front."

"United? You live in Texas. I live in Oklahoma. We're about as united as the Midwest and the West Coast."

He laughed.

"This isn't funny," she warned.

"I know, but some of the ways you draw similarities is actually amusing. We have four weeks to figure out a plan that convinces a judge that we can be parents to Tori."

"Okay, how about if I tell the judge I don't know her birthday or her full name? Will that convince him that I'm parent material?"

He threw her a look that said he was not amused.

"We have a lot of work to do, Ethan, and I'm not convinced we're the best thing for her."

In their present situations, he agreed that they weren't the best thing for Tori. But he had a plan and it included Eve. The major issue would be convincing her to go along with what he suggested.

And he was certain today was not the day to ask.

Chapter Eleven

Eve glanced at the calendar on her desk. They were going into the second week of May. It was four weeks before their court date. If she went, she would have to face her parents. She'd seen them since the accident but not often. The times she had seen them had been difficult. The visits had started with tears and ended with lectures about joining the army. When they'd mentioned her coming home, the conversations had always included how they would take care of her. And she'd always explained that she didn't need to be taken care of.

But her parents were getting older. The realization hit her that no one is guaranteed anything in life.

"Glory, you can go." She turned away from her desk to watch the teenager changing Tori's diaper. "I have to make a phone call and I know that you're excited for your afternoon with Cara."

"Unsupervised," Glory repeated. "Can you believe that? I get a whole afternoon with her. We're going to cuddle, and I'm going to rock her and sing to her. Everything we never get to do."

"Oh, Glory, I'm so happy for you."

Glory jumped up and gave her a hug. It was safe to say Eve hadn't had her personal space invaded this often in years. But she hugged the teenager back.

"Is there anything you need me to do before I go?"

"Can you put her on her blanket so she can play?"

Glory lifted Tori off the sofa and placed her on the activity pad. Of course, the thing that Tori loved the most were the bright pink socks on her feet.

A few minutes later, the door closed softly behind Glory. Eve moved her chair close to the baby, smiling down at her.

"You are beyond precious." Tori smiled up at her. "That's it, I'm coming down there with you."

Eve moved her left foot from the footplate of her chair and followed with the right one. Once they were positioned, she grabbed the frame of her chair and lowered herself to the floor. She scooted so that her back was against the sofa, and then she grabbed the padded seat from her chair and pushed it under her.

"Look at me. Now we're down here together and we can play for a bit."

Tori gurgled and cooed, her hand reaching for Eve. Eve picked the baby up and set her on her lap. She brought her legs up, planting her feet on the floor so that Tori rested against her thighs.

Eve took the baby's hands in hers and clapped them together. "Patty cake, patty cake, baker's man, bake me a cake as fast you can."

She clapped Tori's hands and the baby giggled and tried the gesture on her own.

"Look at you, smart girl. You know, I think I love you very much."

Tori yawned and Eve yawned in return. "Should we take a nap here together? Hmm, I haven't slept on a sofa in a very long time. It's amazing the things you get me to do when you're around. Just like your da…" She shook her head. "Ethan. But he will be your daddy, won't he? He'll make a good daddy."

Tori looked up at her with sleepy eyes.

"You're right, a nap would be good."

She grabbed a bottle off the coffee table that had been moved to the side and tossed it on the sofa. Then she shifted and settled Tori. She was getting pretty good at this. She set the brake on her chair, put a hand on the sofa and one on the frame of her chair. With a good push, she managed to get her seat on the sofa, and then she moved her legs so they stretched out and she leaned against the pillow. Tori eyed her as she pulled the baby up against her, keeping her on the inside.

"This is how we nap." She crossed her right leg over her left and turned toward the baby. "Sleepy time, sweet baby. You've been so sleepy since you had that stomach virus. I need to talk to Carson about that."

In what felt like a few minutes later, she heard someone say, "Hey, Sleeping Beauty, wake up."

Eve startled awake and opened her eyes. "Sierra, what in the world? What day is it?"

"I love those naps when you wake up and you don't know the time or day. Must have been a good one. And Tori is still out."

"She's still getting over the virus."

"It's been six days. She should be over it by now, shouldn't she?"

"Agreed."

"You're getting pretty good at this baby thing." Sierra sat down in the chair next to the sofa.

"Because I have a lot of help."

Sierra arched a brow at that. "No, you're good at this because you're a natural. You were meant to be a mom. I promise, I wouldn't say that to just anyone."

"Meant to be, yeah." She glanced at the chair without meaning to.

"Oh, because paraplegics can't be moms?"

"They can. They are. And I do love her. I can see myself doing this. I've even considered telling Ethan we can find a way to make this work."

"Why not marry him, too?" Sierra said with a sly grin.

"That ship has sailed."

"It can come back into port."

She didn't want to laugh, but she couldn't help herself.

"It's been four years. We've both changed. Too much has happened. And raising Tori would be forever, not a few short days of spending time with her, loving her."

She tried to imagine chasing a toddler through the house, trying to keep her safe.

"Oh, there you go, overthinking this again."

"Easy for you to say," she blurted out.

"Yes, because my life is so easy."

"No, your life isn't easy. But you're amazingly strong. You see everything as an obstacle that can be overcome."

"Right. I'm Miss Optimistic," Sierra said with a roll

of her eyes. "Let's be clear, no one has ever seen me as an optimist. But I am realistic and honest."

"You are both of those things, and a good friend."

"Back to you," Sierra said a moment later with an overly bright smile plastered on her face. "This guy loves you. You love him. This baby needs the two of you. Problem solved."

"Right. It would be a happy life with Ethan giving up his dreams to raise Tori and, on top of that, take care of me. We might be happy for six months, maybe a year, but then he would start thinking about what he missed out on. I don't want to be the choice he resents or the person he marries because he's loyal or because he has a sense of duty." When she added it up, he'd come looking for her only because of Tori. No other reason.

"Stubborn." Sierra stood and took the sleeping child from Eve. "Go get ready for the bonfire. We're taking a wagon to the back field for the nonriders like myself. But I hear you have a horse now."

Eve covered her face with her hands. "You're right. I have a horse."

"Not a dozen roses or a pretty pearl choker, a horse. Because he knows what makes you go all giddy inside. I'm not a romantic but the guy might be worth considering. Go get ready and I'll watch the munchkin."

Eve moved herself over to her chair and released the brakes. "I'm not falling for that."

As she rolled down the hall for her rooms, she thought she heard Sierra chuckle and say, "You're falling for the cowboy."

Eve wouldn't admit it even if she was tortured, but because of Ethan's presence in her life, she took special care with her appearance that night. It had been a long time since she'd done more than pull her dark hair back in a ponytail. Tonight, she left it long and straight, and she found a white hat she'd shoved to the back of her closet. She donned jeans and a long-sleeve plaid shirt over a white T-shirt. And she managed to pull on boots.

When she returned to the living room, Sierra whistled. "You own makeup?"

"Go away." She pulled the baby sling off the table and slid it behind her, then she packed a diaper bag, made two extra bottles and tossed in a container of frozen baby food, specially made by Glory. It was warm outside so it would thaw by the time Tori was ready to eat.

"Ready to go?" Sierra asked. She had changed Tori into a cute sleeper and washed her face. The baby smelled clean.

"Wow, you got her ready to go. Thanks."

"I had younger siblings. It's part of the routine. I'll carry her if you want."

"Go for it."

"She isn't so bad, you know."

Eve studied her friend, looking into hazel eyes that shuttered, keeping out emotion and blocking entrance to even her best friends.

"She's wonderful, actually."

"If my life had been different, maybe I would have wanted babies," Sierra said.

"Maybe you still do."

"No, thank you. I'm not interested in the suffering that comes with marriage. I mean, if you decide on marriage, I'll support you. I'll plan your wedding. I'll be your bridesmaid. Whatever you want. But count me out on romance."

"I'm not planning marriage," Eve assured her friend.

"Thank goodness. I don't want to train a new room-mate. Abby is sweet but she stays in her room most of the time and doesn't say a whole lot."

"She hasn't been out much, has she?"

"Nope."

"Maybe Kylie should pay her a visit?"

Sierra shifted Tori from her right side to her left. "Maybe. She was fixing a sandwich while you were getting ready. She said she'd rather stay inside than face people."

"Safe to say we shouldn't let her stick to herself."

"I thought so myself."

They approached the corral where a flatbed trailer was attached to a truck. Bales of hay around the edges turned it into a hayride. Horses were saddled and tied to the rails of the corral, for those who wanted to ride. Ethan saw them coming and headed in their direction.

"I was going to come and get you," he said as he drew closer.

"I managed to get myself down here." Eve bristled and she knew she shouldn't. He was being kind. He was being chivalrous. And chivalry was a good trait she told herself.

"Meow," Sierra mocked as she settled Tori in her lap.

"Stop," Eve warned her.

Ethan nodded to Sierra and she skipped away, leaving them alone.

"Will I have to apologize each time I sound like I'm taking over or helping too much?" Ethan asked, feeling a little put out by her reaction.

She shook her head. "No, and I'm sorry. I'll try not to be so touchy."

"Thank you. Because I've noticed that you only get touchy with me. I saddled your horse. If you want to ride. I bought a special saddle that has a belt for your waist and straps for your thighs."

She bit down on her bottom lip, and he knew she was fighting a retort, something about his taking over, no doubt. Instead she relaxed. "Thank you," she said. "What about Tori?"

"Kylie is riding on the trailer. She said she'd gladly hold on to Tori because Glory will be there to look after Cara."

"Sounds like a plan." She started to move away from him. "My chair. I want it stowed in the back of the truck. When we get to the bonfire, I want to be able to move freely on my own."

"Of course."

He hadn't thought about that, but she was right.

"Evie!" a little girl called out and headed their way, Kylie hurrying after her.

"That's Maggie. You've met, haven't you?" Eve asked him.

"Yes, briefly."

"Evie," Maggie yelled and climbed onto Eve's lap without hesitation.

"Hey, Maggie sweetest. I haven't seen you in way too long."

Maggie giggled. "At church on Sunday."

"That's waaay too long. That's five whole days."

"Monday, Tuesday, Wednesday, Thursday, Friday." Maggie counted the days off on her fingers. "That's five."

"Yep."

Maggie leaned close. "I heard you're going to ride a horse and we're going to hold Tori."

"I know."

Kylie reached for Tori. "I'll take these two. You two go get ready."

Eve drew in a breath and nodded. "Let's do this."

Ethan leaned down and her arms went around his neck. He lifted her from her chair and carried her to the waiting horse. He wouldn't admit it but he'd ridden the horse hard for an hour, just to make sure it was ready for this ride. Her solo ride.

"You're tense. Worried?" she asked him. "It was your idea."

"I know."

She hugged him tighter and put her face close to his. "I've got this, Ethan. You don't have to worry. You'll be right there with me."

"I know."

"So relax." She kissed his cheek.

"I'm relaxed." He turned his head just slightly, touching his lips to hers.

"Did that help?" she teased as he pulled back.

"Immensely." He lifted her, seating her on the gelding. Twister didn't move a muscle.

This time she slid her booted right foot into the stirrup.

"You're a pro at this."

She pushed her left foot into the stirrup. "The internet is a wonderful thing."

He laughed as he handed her the reins, then showed her how to use the straps for her legs. The higher back on the saddle would give her more support and a belt that went around her waist. Everything had Velcro for quick removal. Once he had her situated, he grabbed her wheelchair and headed for the truck.

"You really think this is a good idea?" Isaac West asked, following him to the truck.

"Of course it is," Ethan answered. He didn't mind that the other man was protective.

"What if something happens?"

Ethan set the chair in the back of Jack's truck. "She's an experienced rider."

"Who can't feel anything from the waist down."

"And I'm a grown man who will be right there with her. She loves to ride. She should be able to do what she loves."

Isaac raised a hand and said, "You're the boss."

"No, I'm not. But I am the man who…" Loves her? Yeah, he still loved her.

Isaac grinned. "It isn't as if you're keeping *that* a secret."

"Better get our horses," Ethan said, ending the discussion. He had picked a horse from the many owned by Mercy Ranch, a big chestnut gelding that fit his taller stature. The horse didn't seem to like him overly much, rolling his eyes every time Ethan got close.

"What horse are you riding?" Eve asked when he returned to her side.

"The chestnut over there."

She laughed. "No, you're not."

"Yeah, I am. Why?"

"Because you don't want to ride that horse. No one wants to ride that horse."

"I like him. He's big."

"Suit yourself. Just hold on tight."

He pushed his hat up and gave her a look. "You doubt me?"

"Nope, I just know what they're up to."

She meant Isaac and the others. He turned his gaze to the horse. "Okay, I will."

"And lead him off away from the rest of us," she warned.

"I don't plan on getting thrown," he told her. "But if you have a few pointers, that would be nice."

She backed her horse away from him and he was pleased to see how well the Arabian responded to the reins. "Don't use spurs. Hold the reins tight. Don't give him an in.

"Got it. I'll catch up with you." He tipped his hat and went to get his mount. He led the horse away from the others, all of whom were on their horses and ready to go.

The gelding danced a little as Ethan tried to get his foot in the stirrup. He held the reins tight and ran a hand down the horse's neck.

"Easy there, big guy. Hold up." He said the latter in a firm voice.

He was very aware of everyone watching him.

After a minute, the horse calmed. He got his left foot in the stirrup, swung his right leg over the horse's back and settled into the saddle. The horse immediately began to buck. Great. He took Eve's advice and held tight, keeping the reins tight but not so tight the horse would fight and rear up on him.

After a few minutes the gelding settled, shook as if he might attempt to shake his rider, then he ambled back to the other horses as if to say, "Nothing to see here, go about your business."

Eve clapped and a few of the others joined in.

"That was like a Saturday night at the rodeo." She laughed and he thought about kissing her again.

As if she could read his thoughts, her smile instantly dissolved.

"So I take it he's the horse they put all of the new guys on?"

"You picked him," Isaac said as he rode past.

"You could have warned me."

Isaac pushed his hat back on his head a bit. "Nah, that wouldn't be any fun. And I never put a guy on there that I think can't handle him."

"Oh, so I should take this as a compliment."

"And a warning," Isaac spoke quietly, then he gave his horse a nudge and cantered off to catch up with the hayride trailer.

It was an hour ride to the site of the bonfire. Ethan remained close to Eve, making sure the gelding gave her no trouble.

"You can relax," she told him after a while. "The horse is good. I'm good. I can't believe how much I missed this. Ethan, I mean it when I say thank you. I don't know that I ever would have taken this chance if you hadn't pushed."

He knew better than to respond.

She laughed a little. "Oh, smart man, not commenting."

"I do learn, eventually."

"So do I. Eventually." She leaned a little in the saddle and clucked to the horse. The gray listened and broke from an easy trot to a slow, rhythmic canter.

Ethan watched for a moment, mesmerized and more

than a little bit in love. And then he realized anything could happen and it would be his fault. He gave his horse a nudge and caught up with her. She eased back on the reins.

"Did I scare you?" she asked.

"Not at all."

"Liar."

"Okay, then. You scared me a lot."

She threw back her head and laughed. "But it was so much fun."

He exhaled. "For you, maybe."

Up ahead he could see the bonfire. The truck and trailer were already there, and some of the men were getting chairs set up, pulling coolers from the truck bed and adding wood to the fire. A short distance from the fire he spotted a screened canopy and inside were Kylie and the children.

Eve brought her horse to a halt at a round pen where other horses were tied. She waited for him to tie his horse and help her.

She pulled her right leg to the left side of the horse, leaned down to wrap her arms around his neck and he lifted her down from the saddle. He held her there for a moment, deciding his next move. There was music playing from a truck radio and he didn't immediately carry her to the chair that waited nearby.

"We can still dance," he told her.

"We what?"

"You used that as one of your arguments. We will never dance together. But we can."

"Ethan…" But as he twirled her around to the old country song, she stopped complaining.

"When did you become such a romantic?" she asked when the song ended.

"I always was but a younger man is more inclined to brashness and avoiding his inner romantic. They're afraid someone will make fun of them."

"Because you were always the guy that people made fun of?"

"Never." He tucked a strand of hair behind her ear, then kissed that sweet spot where she smelled of herbal shampoo and lavender.

"We should join the others," she whispered, turning her head away from his. But he knew, with her in his arms, that they were still connected. There was still a chance.

He had arrived in Hope with the idea that he was still angry with her, that he couldn't trust her. But the more time he spent with her, the more he realized he would spend the rest of his life courting her if it meant he had even the slightest chance of getting her back.

He wanted to kiss her, but he realized they had an audience. With that in mind, he carried her to the circle of light around the bonfire.

He settled her in her chair and then he went in search of a lawn chair to sit next to her. But first he headed to the canopy where Kylie had the children, including Tori. When the baby girl saw him, she smiled. It was the kind of smile that made everything better. It reminded him that everything he was doing mattered.

"How is she?" he asked Kylie as he picked Tori up off the blanket spread out on the floor of the enclosure.

"She had fun on the hayride. She sat on my lap but she really loves Maggie."

The four-year-old smiled up at him as she changed her doll's diaper. "I'm good with babies."

"I bet you are." He glanced around. "Do you have her blanket? I thought I'd take her so she can sit with Eve and me."

"Yes, it's right here with her bag." Kylie picked both up and handed them to him. "You're pretty good at this."

"I'm glad you think so. Most of the time I feel like I'm going under and there isn't a life preserver in sight."

"That's how parenting feels about half the time," she said with a grin. "But you'll get the hang of it. I came into this without a lot of experience. But if you love them, you figure it out."

"Does she feel warm to you? Maybe it's just the night, the fire?"

Kylie kissed Tori's forehead. "I get a better read that way. My hand isn't always a good indicator. And yes, she does feel warm. Maybe talk to Carson. She should have been over that virus by now. Hopefully she isn't catching something else. Babies do get sick, Ethan. She'll be fine."

"Another thing I wasn't prepared for." He shifted her in his arms so that her head rested on his shoulder. "Thank you."

"Anytime." She held her hand out to Maggie. "Come on, kiddo, let's go find your dad and Andy."

Maggie was all for that and gave Kylie a tug toward the opening. Ethan followed, holding Tori close. This wasn't how he expected to start a family but it was his path now and he didn't know any other way.

People were circled around the fire pit, laughing and talking. Some were roasting hot dogs, others stood at the nearby table where all of the fixings were spread out. He searched the group and spotted Eve near Glory and the young cowboy Kenny. He paused, eavesdropping as Glory tried to convince Kenny they should go out and he told her he had plans to be a physical therapist and as much as he liked her, he thought she needed to grow up a little before she started dating.

Glory shrugged it off with a smile but it didn't take much to see that the smile was plastered on.

Ouch. Ethan would have to talk to the younger man about being more subtle with women. He could see the hurt on Glory's face. Eve saw it, too, and put a hand on her arm, whispering something to comfort her. Glory laughed.

Eve turned, saw him with Tori and smiled. The fire danced in the fire pit, giving her skin a warm glow. As he drew closer, she held out her arms to Tori.

For the first time in four years, he had hope.

He thought about the ranch house he'd made an offer on. A big sprawling place that was already handicap accessible. He'd wanted to tell Eve about the place. More than once he'd nearly mentioned the stable, the land or some other feature but then he'd stopped himself.

He had an unsettled feeling, as if telling her would undo something amazing that was happening between them. What if she had no intention of joining him in raising Tori? Worse, what if she didn't want to resume their relationship?

Hope was a fragile thing but he wasn't giving up. He had a six-month-old reason to keep trying.

Plus his own heart refused to let go.

Chapter Twelve

The phone rang as Eve opened her car door. It was Monday and she was meeting Kylie for their weekly lunch. It had been two weeks since their last lunch. Two weeks since Ethan had arrived in Hope with Tori. In that time she'd become somewhat of an expert at getting herself out of the car, and then unhooking Tori from her car seat and pulling her out. It wasn't easy, but she was learning. She was also discovering arm and back muscles she didn't realize she had. Her workouts hadn't prepared her for this.

After getting Tori settled on her lap, she glanced at her phone. Her parents. They hadn't called in weeks so she could only guess that they'd heard about James and Hanna. When the phone rang again, she actually answered it.

"Hi, Mom." Tori smiled up at her, content now on Eve's lap.

"Eve, honey, I'm so glad you answered." Eve's mother, Darlene, sounded older. When had that happened?

"I know, Mom." Eve stopped on the sidewalk. "I know about James and Hanna."

"Oh, honey, I am so sorry. I wish I'd known sooner. It's been a month, I believe. I just saw Ethan Forester's mother at the store and she told me about the accident. She also told me about the guardianship thing. I'm so sorry."

"I'm okay, Mom. I'm…" She sighed. "I'm heartbroken. I regret so much and the four years I've lost. I can't get back the time, the moments that I should have had."

As she said the words, it all became real in a way it hadn't been before that moment. Saying the words out loud changed everything. She had run from her life, from the people who loved her. Why? Because of that, she'd lost two people she truly cared about. And she'd lost four years with her parents.

"Mom, I'm going to be coming to Texas soon. For the custody hearing."

"And you'll stay with us. Of course you'll stay with us."

"Mom, the hearing is in Dallas. I'll have to stay there."

"We could drive you…" Her mom sighed. "I'm doing it again, aren't I?"

Eve found it easier to laugh. "Yes, but it's okay."

"Now that you're a mom, you'll understand how hard it is to let go. You'll want to fix everything for that little girl and make everything better for her."

"She isn't…" She started to say the words but then she couldn't. The child in her arms needed to be someone's little girl.

Her mom waited, not interrupting the silence. For which Eve was thankful.

"Mom, I would like for you to be there for the hearing. I'll give you more information when I have it."

"What about Ethan?" her mom asked.

"What about him?"

"Will you work out your relationship?"

"I don't know. We'll have to figure out a way to raise her, to share custody."

"I understand you don't want me to interfere." Darlene's tone was hesitant. "But I am your mother. I know you're grown and independent but you loved that boy and I don't think you ever stopped loving him. He's a good man."

"Yes, he is."

"Then what's the problem?"

"I'm afraid, Mom." She finally said the words she'd thought in her head but hadn't really found a way to voice. "I'm afraid he'll take over my life. I'm afraid that I'll become the person he takes care of, makes decisions for, and I just can't do that."

"I know that's how you feel." Of course her mom knew, she was a caseworker and therapist. "And it can happen. But you can prevent it, stop it, without shutting people out."

"Is that what I did to you?" Eve asked, knowing it was time to clear the air between herself and her parents.

"We overreacted, Eve. And so did you. You made choices we didn't understand and then you were injured and we wanted to fix it all."

"I know." And she understood, she really did. "Mom,

I have to go. I have a friend waiting for me and I'm sitting in front of the café with a baby."

"Oh, of course you should go. But before you go, honey, your dad went to church last week. He wants me to go, too. I'm just not quite ready yet."

"Church?" Wow, that was huge. "Is everything okay?"

Her mother laughed at that. "Everything is fine. Oh, I think he's getting old and thinking about life and what comes next. It's a phase."

"A phase?"

"Well, maybe not a phase. I don't think he'll grow out of it. He said he grew up going to church and then he went through that phase where he questioned everything. Now he's questioning again. You'd think he was seventeen and not seventy. Well, you go have lunch with your friend. We'll talk soon."

"Mom, I love you."

"I love you, too, Evie."

Eve ended the call and pushed her way up the ramp to Holly's. The door opened and Holly held it wide for her.

"Everything okay?" Holly asked.

"My mom. And yes, they're fine. Is Kylie here?"

"Yep, she's waiting for you."

Eve maneuvered through the crowded café that now boasted the sign HOLLY'S. She was so happy for her friend that this business was now officially named after her.

"What's for dessert today?" Eve asked as she approached the table where Kylie waited.

Holly looked offended. "You know my desserts are good."

"Oh, they're the best," Eve agreed. "Except that one you made with the mint. That was weird, Holly."

The café owner laughed. "I like to experiment. Today we have cheesecake, apple pie and brownies."

"The brownies have cherries in them," Kylie chimed in.

"They're good," Holly insisted.

"I'm sure they are," Kylie answered. "But I think I'll stick with cheesecake. And I'll have the chicken alfredo."

"Salad for me," Eve told her. "And nothing for Tori. She still isn't feeling well."

"It's been a week!" Kylie gave the baby girl a worried look. "What's going on with her?"

"I don't know. She's feverish and just listless. She seemed to be doing better, and then maybe she got a secondary virus while her immune system was weak?"

Eve unwrapped the baby and handed her to Kylie, who'd situated Cara in her car seat so she could take Tori. "What's up with you, baby girl?"

Tori smiled a little but she didn't respond the way she would have before the virus. Her eyes looked weepy and her cheeks were flushed.

"I should have noticed sooner, shouldn't I?" Eve moved a little closer to Kylie and Tori. "She's really sick and I had no idea why. She's been miserable and I should have called Carson."

"She's fine, Eve. Babies get sick. We'll just call Carson and find out if he can see her after lunch. You should let Ethan know that we're taking her to the doctor."

Eve felt a sense of dread in the pit of her stomach. "I'm so sorry, Tori."

"Give her a hug and a smile and relax. If it's a virus, viruses run their course. And if it's something bacterial, Carson will give her antibiotics and she'll be back to her happy, smiling self in no time."

An hour later Eve and Kylie were sitting in the waiting room of Carson's clinic waiting for him to examine Tori. The outer door opened, letting in the sounds of summer—traffic on the road, a mower in the distance and children laughing as they played in a nearby yard.

Ethan pulled off his white cowboy hat as he approached, his concerned gaze falling on Tori. He sat in a chair across from them.

"What's going on?" he asked.

Eve held Tori close, comforting her as she fussed and refused her bottle. "She's sick again. Or maybe she didn't get over the stomach virus. Kylie thought it would be better if Carson examined her."

"I think that's a good idea." He smiled at Tori. "What's up, little chick, aren't you feeling good?"

Tori cried and reached for him. The gesture clearly moved him and Eve felt the sting of tears in her eyes as she handed the baby to Ethan. He wasn't completely dry-eyed himself. Tori had changed their lives. She was no longer responsible only for herself, her own welfare, her own happiness.

Carson's nurse, Jenna, appeared in the door. "You can bring Tori back now." She looked at the crowd. "Maybe not all of you."

Kylie motioned for Ethan to go. "Go with Eve. The two of you make her feel safe. I'll wait here with Cara."

Ethan motioned Eve ahead of him and he carried Tori. They followed the nurse down a fluorescent-lit hallway to an exam room. Carson was already waiting for them. He turned from his computer and pulled off black wire-framed glasses.

"I'm sorry to hear that Tori is still sick." He closed the door and then he sat down, pulling his stool closer to the three of them. "I'm going to check her temperature, then her eyes, ears, the basics and we'll go from there. Odds are it's just a second round of another virus. It happens."

He ran the thermometer across her brow and frowned. "That's a little higher than I expected but nothing out of the ordinary. 102.5."

Eve inhaled, and watched as Carson continued his examination. The basics, as he had told them. Eyes, ears, nose, he even got a peek at her throat.

He pulled the stethoscope up, placing the ear tips in his ears. He rubbed the bell and, before placing it on her chest, let Tori look at it. He listened, moving the bell of the stethoscope from place to place and then to her back. Eve clenched and unclenched her fists as she watched his expression change.

"Carson?" she finally spoke because she couldn't take it any longer. She'd known this man for over a year. She knew his smiles, his frowns, his concern.

He sighed and sat back on the stool. He looked from Tori to Ethan and then to Eve. His gray eyes were somber.

"I'm convinced she does have a virus but, as often

happens during a routine examination, I clearly hear a heart murmur. It's possible it was previously diagnosed. Ethan, do you have any medical records?"

He shook his head. "I don't and I never thought about it. She's healthy and hasn't been sick and I didn't think about medical records."

"We'll need to see if we can find something. There should be records on her immunizations, too."

"What do we do?" Eve asked, reaching for Tori. She needed to hold her, comfort her. Comfort herself.

"First we relax," Carson said with a calming smile.

"Relax?"

Carson grew serious again. "Eve, relax. That's exactly what I mean. Yes, a heart defect is serious. But there are degrees of serious. There are murmurs that are found in infancy that the child grows out of. There are murmurs that are mild. And some require surgery or other medical intervention."

"What kind is this?"

"The kind that requires a specialist to look at because I'm a trauma surgeon turned family doctor. I don't have the experience or training to give you a diagnosis. I also don't have the medical equipment necessary. She needs to see a specialist in Tulsa, one who will do an echocardiogram."

"Okay, how do we get an appointment with this specialist?" she asked.

"I'll make a few calls and get you an appointment. Until then, I am going to start her on a round of antibiotics."

"Thank you." Eve held Tori closer than ever, until the baby squirmed to get loose.

"Eve, she's going to be okay. She's a typically healthy almost seven-month-old. If I saw a reason for real concern, I would tell you."

She nodded. "I know. I do know that. I just can't…"

"You won't," he assured her with a quick hug.

Eve didn't complain when Ethan took the handles of her chair and pushed her back to the waiting room and to Kylie. When she saw them walk through the door, Kylie stood. Her gaze flicked past Eve to Carson.

"A heart murmur," Eve told her friend. "She needs to see a specialist."

"Then she will see a specialist," Kylie confirmed. "And she'll be fine. I know she'll be fine."

Eve kissed Tori's soft, baby cheek and felt a hand, firm and comforting, settled on her shoulder. They were a family. Maybe they hadn't planned this but the three of them were a family. It felt right and it felt frightening all at the same time.

It also felt not quite real.

Ethan pushed Eve's chair to her car while she kept Tori held close, as if she feared the child would evaporate. He wanted to comfort her but he didn't know the words that would make this better. He was afraid if he pushed, she would withdraw from him. After all, isn't that what she did when she hit an obstacle?

"Eve, we're both worried. But we have to trust that this situation isn't a surprise to God and we also know that Carson isn't taking chances. He said it could be minor, something she'll grow out of."

"I know that." She opened the back door of her car and lifted Tori into the car seat. The baby whined a little. "I was thinking about the verse, about all things working together for good for those that trust God. I want to have faith but I also want to yell because why this baby? Hasn't she been through enough?"

"Yes, she's been through enough. You've been through enough, too. Storms don't stop coming just because we've had enough rain."

"Nice analogy. I'm just tired of storms."

"We can rest in the fact that He's a refuge in the storm."

"Does your faith ever waver?" she asked.

"Of course my faith wavers, Eve. Do you think I'm made of stone and all of this hasn't affected me? You broke my heart."

He hadn't meant to say it. It seemed like the least effective argument. Plus he couldn't help but think that a man didn't just open up and tell a woman that she'd knocked him down emotionally. But it was too late to take it back now.

"I'm sorry," she said, backing up to close the door of her car. "I didn't mean to break your heart. Or mine. I'd convinced myself that mine was the only broken heart. I was the only one hurting. I didn't think about your pain. For that I am truly sorry and I hope you can forgive me."

"I forgave you a long time ago."

"It's good, for us to talk. This way we can clear the air and focus our attention on Tori and what she needs from us."

"I agree, she needs us fully committed to her happiness."

She opened her car door and transferred herself inside, then reached over and quickly took the wheels off her chair and hauled the three pieces over her lap to place them in the passenger seat.

Watching her, he thought that maybe she'd been right to distance herself from him. He did want to do everything for her, even now. He wanted to ease her way, make her life less complicated. If he could do more than pray, he would chase away the storms so that she never had to deal with another thing that shook her world.

"Stop looking so serious, cowboy." She smiled up at him, a glimmer of her old self. Her expression teased and her dark eyes flashed with humor.

"What makes you think I'm serious?" But he was, of course. And his attempt at lightness fell flat.

"That's the face a man wears when he's about to fight a bull and win. A woman likes to know her man will fight those battles for her." She reached for his hand. "I always knew you'd win any battle, Ethan. You're that determined. Don't try to conquer me. Please."

"You've got my word."

Her laughter shattered the stillness and even Tori giggled a little. "You know that isn't a promise you can keep. It's a part of who you are. You have to conquer enemies and save us all."

"This isn't a conversation I can win." He leaned over and kissed her, just once. And then, on second thought, he kissed her again. "I do like to win."

She pulled back and reached for her car door. "I know you do. But right now, you have to conquer the pharmacy in Grove and get that prescription for Tori."

He glanced at his watch. "I guess I'd better get on the road. I'll bring you the prescription as soon as I get it."

"Thank you."

Ethan closed her door and then watched as she pulled out of the parking lot. He allowed a slow grin to spread across his face as he watched her go.

"That's the smile of a man who thinks he's won a victory."

He turned, laughing just a little because Kylie West had managed to sneak up on him. "I thought you were inside talking to your husband."

"I was, but he has patients and I need to get Cara home. The other two kids will be getting out of school in an hour and Cara needs a nap before the chaos. Carson said he's confident the murmur is mild, by the way."

"I'm glad. That makes me feel better. She's so young to have to go through so much."

"Yes, she is. But she has the two of you, and Carson will make sure she sees the best pediatric cardiologist. But that smile was the smile of a man who thinks things are going his way."

He adjusted his hat on his head and thought about the best way to answer that question. "I bought a place about thirty minutes from Hope."

"Uh-oh. You're not a conqueror. You're a man who needs advice."

He rubbed his chin. "I wouldn't have thought so until you said that. Do I need advice?"

"You've known Eve longer than I have," she conceded. "But I know the Eve that survived a bombing and paralysis. I know that Eve doesn't like surprises. Even if they're good surprises. She likes to be in control of her life, her future, her choices."

He started to explain that now Eve's choices directly affected Tori's life. But that was an argument he wouldn't win.

"I didn't say she's right," Kylie said, giving him a sympathetic look.

"No, I guess you didn't."

"I'd encourage you to not give up." She gave him a conspiratorial wink. "She needs her life shaken up a little. Sometimes we get too comfortable and we stop moving forward."

"Thank you for that."

"Me?" She pointed to herself. "Did I say something? I don't remember saying anything. See you later, Ethan."

"Yes, later." He tipped his hat, the way his dad had told him a gentleman should.

The drive to Grove gave him time to think about what direction he needed to take with Eve. Because he did plan on taking their relationship in a certain direction. He was determined to win, but realized that was the wrong tactic to take when trying to win a woman's heart. It wasn't about winning, it was about being on the same team.

The winning team, he told himself. It wasn't bad to win. Especially with the woman you want to spend your life with.

Chapter Thirteen

"I'm not going to lie and tell you I'm not worried," Eve told Ethan as they started up the elevator at the pediatric care facility.

Ethan held Tori so Eve pushed the button for the fourth floor.

"I'm nervous but I'm not really worried. No matter what, this is treatable. She's going to be fine, either with or without a procedure. Carson assured us of that, and he got her in with one of the best doctors in the state."

"I know." She leaned back, taking deep breaths to relax. She smiled up at Tori. The little girl was definitely feeling better. Since Monday she'd perked up, started eating again and was sleeping much better.

"Looking at her now, it's hard to believe she's sick," Ethan said.

"I know, that's what I was thinking. But what if she hadn't gotten sick? When would we have noticed that she has a heart murmur?"

The elevator doors slid open and she rolled out ahead of Ethan. A woman smiled at Ethan and Tori, greeted him, then skimmed an awkward gaze over Eve. The woman hurried onto the elevator.

They entered the cardiologist's office and Eve approached the new-patient desk. The receptionist looked past her to Ethan.

"Could I help you?"

Ethan didn't respond. Eve glanced back at him and saw that he had heard, he simply wasn't going to answer. She couldn't help but smile at him before turning to face the receptionist.

"Can I help you?" the woman asked again.

Eve drew in a breath and reminded herself that the woman wasn't being intentionally rude. She just wasn't thinking. She wasn't seeing Eve, she was seeing the wheelchair. For some reason that made people uncomfortable. It made them skim past her, overlook her and direct questions to the person standing next to her.

"We have an appointment for Tori Garner." She hadn't ever called Tori by her full name. She'd just been Tori. All of this time she'd been this little person who belonged to someone else.

"You're her parents?" the receptionist asked, studying the computer screen.

"Guardians," Eve responded.

"Do you have legal guardianship?"

Ethan pulled a paper from his pocket. "We do."

He handed it over and the receptionist took it, glanced at it and handed it back.

"I'll need you to fill out these forms. The nurse will call you when they're ready to see you. Please have a seat on that side of the waiting room."

Eve took the clipboard with the paperwork from

the receptionist, smiled at the woman as pleasantly as she possibly could and turned away from the desk. Ethan followed her to the waiting area. As she started to fill out the paperwork, he watched. After a minute he cleared his throat. She ignored him and filled out the last pages. He cleared his throat again.

"What do you want?"

"Do people always do that?" he asked.

"Do what?" She knew what he meant but didn't want to discuss it.

"Bypass you? Look away? Ignore you?"

"Not always, but some people do react that way. They see the chair and I'm not sure what they assume. I handle it. I know the chair makes them uncomfortable. If they'd understand that the chair is to me as legs are to you, maybe they would relax."

"I never thought about that."

She hesitated, then answered. "Because you didn't have to think about it. Neither did I until I became the person in this chair. I remember my first experience at an appointment. I was sitting in the waiting room and this guy walks by, and I guess he wanted something behind me. Instead of the normal 'Excuse me, can I get in here?' he said, 'I'm just going to move you over here.' Move me? As if I couldn't move myself. Would you do that to an able-bodied person? 'Hey lady, I'm going to pick you up and move you.' No, you wouldn't."

The words poured out and she realized that she'd grown louder than she intended. "Oops."

"Don't apologize," Ethan told her. "I needed to know this. I want you to never be afraid to tell me things. And if I mess up, tell me."

"You never have to worry about that."

"I know I don't." He reached for the clipboard. "Want me to take that up to her?"

"Nope."

She took the paperwork back to the receptionist, thanked her and returned to Ethan and Tori. He'd given the baby a cracker and she was happily gumming the treat while watching a movie on the TV hanging from the wall.

"I'm worried," Eve admitted.

"So am I. But I've been doing research and I know that whatever we find today, she'll be okay."

Yes, they would be okay. And Tori would be okay. Eve thought back a month, when it was just her living a life with no one really counting on her. What a difference a few short weeks could make in a person's life.

Never in her wildest imagination would she have pictured herself here with Ethan, with Tori, sharing this moment.

Thirty minutes they were sitting in the doctor's office as he explained Tori's heart defect and tests he wanted to do. Eve listened as he explained a balloon procedure that could be used to stretch the valve if necessary.

"At this point, I'm hopeful that we won't need to worry about that. But we'll do regular checkups. If she ever has surgery or dental work done, make sure your pediatrician gives antibiotics prior to the procedures."

Eve sat back, swamped with relief and a need to hold Tori. She held her arms out and Ethan handed her over. She settled the baby girl on her lap, holding her close. As if she could hold her close enough to protect her from all harm.

"You may push," she told Ethan as they left the office. "Right now I just need to hold her."

"I know."

Did his voice sound a little choked? She looked back at him. They were at the elevator and she realized she wanted to reach for his hand. She wanted his strength. She wanted his touch. As he pushed her through the elevator doors, she reached for him. He smiled, disarming her completely.

"We survived our first real parenting crisis." He gave her hand a light squeeze as the elevator doors opened. "I need to show you something."

"What?"

"It's a surprise."

She allowed him to push her across the parking lot to his truck. He took Tori and buckled her into her car seat, then lifted Eve from her chair and placed her in the passenger seat.

"I don't like surprises," she told him.

He stood in the door of the truck, close. His scent surrounded her, outdoorsy and fresh. He'd left his hat in the truck for the doctor's appointment and there was the slightest indention in his hair where the hat had been. She reached out, touching his dark auburn hair. It was more brown than red, straight and fine to the touch. She slid her fingers to the back of his head and pulled him close, kissing him.

He pulled back from her. "Eve, you have to stop doing that. I'm supposed to be the one surprising you."

"I do my best to keep you guessing," she told him, smiling.

"I'm going to close the door now because if I don't, I'm going to kiss you again."

"Chicken," she called out as he closed the door.

Five minutes later, they were navigating Tulsa traffic and heading northeast toward Hope. Tori jabbered for a bit, then fell asleep. Eve could think of dozens of things to say but she remained quiet, needing time to think, to get her thoughts straight.

They were outside Vinita when he took a right-hand turn south, in the wrong direction. She let him go for a few miles because far be it for a woman to interfere with a man's driving skills.

"You know you're going the wrong direction, right?"

"Yep," he answered. "Actually, I'm going in the right direction for where we're headed."

"Do I need to remind you that I don't like surprises?"

"I think you'll like this one."

He made a left turn onto a paved driveway. She was surprised when he hit a button on his visor and the gates at the end of the driveway swung open. In response, her stomach tightened because a man wouldn't be able to activate a gate if he didn't have the power to do so.

The drive was a quarter of a mile, lined on both sides by white vinyl fencing. In the distance she could see a tree-dotted lawn and glimpses of a home. Eventually it came into view, a brick ranch-style home, large and sprawling with a wide, covered front porch, manicured lawn and well-maintained flower gardens.

"What's going on?" Her heart was beating fast, and she hated the feeling of being trapped.

She couldn't escape this situation. She couldn't get out and walk away. She had no power. He hadn't intentionally taken it, but he had it nonetheless. She was trapped in this truck with no way out.

The anxiety pounded at her until it hurt to breathe. She hadn't experienced a panic attack in so long. This shouldn't cause one. It was a surprise, nothing more. It was a house. Just a house. But she didn't like surprises. Or helplessness.

"I know, you already told me that," he responded.

She must have said it out loud. She put her hand on the window control and took a deep breath as fresh air blew through the cab of the truck. *Breathe*, she told herself. *Just breathe.*

She closed her eyes and images flashed through her mind, of being on the side of a dirt road in Afghanistan, unable to move, unable to call for help or to get to the men and woman who had been in the vehicle with her. Scattered pieces of metal littered the surrounding area. She could hear someone call for help. She couldn't move.

"Eve?" Ethan's voice, loud, too loud.

She opened her eyes, shaking her head as she did. She didn't want him to talk. Not right now. She needed a minute to be calm, to pray. God would give her victory over the fear. She'd told herself that numerous times. Her brain told her that God could. Her heart sometimes didn't agree.

She prayed for peace. She prayed for him to take the fear—the sense of helplessness—away.

"I'm fine," she whispered. More to herself than to him.

"Are you?" he asked.

She shook her head. "I just need a minute. I don't want to be here. I want to go back to Hope. I do not want to be stranded out here, in your truck, unable to get to where I want to be."

It was irrational, she knew that. But fear couldn't always be rationalized. It just was. And fear wasn't of God. Fear was a reaction and not always relative to a situation. She wanted to explain that to him. It wasn't his fault. It wasn't about the surprise. It was that moment, when she felt she couldn't escape. For some reason the fear convinced her there was no escape, that she was trapped.

"It isn't your fault," she whispered, hoping he understood.

Kylie had told her to memorize Psalm 34:4. *I sought the Lord and He heard me, and delivered me from all of my fears.* She repeated it in her mind as she took deep breaths, and eventually her heart returned to its normal rhythm.

"You don't like surprises," he repeated. His expression, when she looked at him, was troubled.

"No, I don't." She could trust him with her fears. She knew that. "I don't like to feel stuck, as if I can't get away." She took another deep breath. "It's because of the accident. No, it wasn't an accident. It was an attack. And I couldn't get away. I was conscious, unable to move, unable to escape or to help my friends."

"Helpless," he said. "I am so sorry, Eve."

"It's okay."

"No, it isn't. It isn't okay that it happened to you. It isn't okay that I didn't know or understand."

She put a hand up to stop his apologies. "These attacks seldom happen and when they do, there's no predicting or understanding. But I know how to fight my way out so they don't totally consume me."

"Okay, but from now on, I'll pay more attention," he said as his hand moved to cover hers.

"So what is the surprise?"

"Can we get out?" he asked.

"Sure, of course." She waited as he got out.

He opened her door and she allowed him to lift her out of the truck and set her in her chair. She positioned her feet and released the brake while he got Tori out of her seat.

The lawn was flat and smooth and easily navigated. As they got closer, she could see that a ramp led to the wide, concrete front porch. The front door was wide and had no step. The house was obviously handicap accessible. Ethan unlocked the door and opened it for her.

She wasn't surprised that he had a key. Before going in, she glanced out at the fields, empty of livestock.

Ethan waited. She gave her wheels a push and entered the home. The floor plan was open, with floor-to-ceiling windows, wide doors, a handicap-accessible kitchen. The back patio was accessible by a ramp.

If she had planned a house, it would look like this one.

"What's going on?"

"I bought it." His tone said this was the most perfect idea in the world.

"Oh, good. You'll be living close to Hope."

He frowned at that.

She ignored his frown and went out the back door to the patio.

* * *

Ethan looked from Eve to Tori. "Women are complicated creatures."

Tori smiled and wiped her nose on his shoulder.

"Exactly," he told the baby. "You act like you're going to cuddle, but instead you use me for a tissue. I kiss her and she acts as if this is exactly what was meant to be, and now this."

He stood for a moment watching as she headed for a chicken coop that needed chickens and then he headed that way, needing to find a way to put this to rights.

"I've messed up, haven't I?" he asked the baby.

Tori obviously didn't answer. Her head rested on his chest and he snuggled her close. "Let's go see if there's any hope."

He met her on her way back to the house. She pushed the wheels with all of her might and he pictured her as a teenager, stomping away from him when he'd said something stupid.

"What do you think?" he asked.

She eyed him suspiciously for a moment, then stopped. "It's a beautiful place."

He sat down on the glider bench so they could talk at eye level. But then he didn't know what to say. He'd had it all planned. He knew what he wanted to say and how. He'd thought this would be the perfect place. He had convinced himself that if he showed her this place that she would want to be a part of his life, of Tori's. Permanently.

"I bought this house because I thought it made sense for us, for Tori."

Her eyes widened. "Is this a proposal?"

He shrugged. "I guess so. But now I'm thinking I had this all wrong. I want to marry you, Eve. I've always wanted to marry you. This isn't just about providing a family for Tori, it's about us, our dreams and the plans we had for our future."

"But we're not doing the six kids or the horse training. And I'm not leaving Hope. It's my home. My friends are there. My life is there."

"This house is less than thirty miles from Hope," he offered.

"But this isn't my home. Tori is ours. There's no doubt about that. And we can come up with a solution together." She moved a little closer. "*Together.* Not you making decisions for us that you think are best."

He left the ring in his pocket.

She was right, he didn't know her as well as he once had. He didn't understand her life. He'd brought her here to surprise her and instead he'd caused a panic attack.

He didn't know what to say now that she'd shared her feelings with him. He'd bought a house, planned a life together that she didn't want.

"It's always going to be about that horse, isn't it?" he asked. "If I'd known how that would change everything, I would have kept out of it."

"But you couldn't know. Neither could I. If I hadn't gone in the army. If I hadn't gotten injured. The horse wouldn't have mattered. It would have been a chapter but not the turning point. If everything hadn't changed, I would have looked at this home and fallen more in love with you. But the person I am today, I need to be involved in decisions."

"If it makes a difference," he said. "I'm sorry. And I love you."

Tori shifted in his arms, reaching for a butterfly that flitted past. After a minute he stood, knowing that retreat was sometimes a sound strategy.

"We should go."

She touched his hand. "I'm sorry."

"Me, too."

Chapter Fourteen

For a week, Ethan gave Eve the space she seemed to need. Or maybe he was just afraid of what she would tell him if they sat down to talk. They still shared responsibility for Tori, but Eve had made up a schedule. His days, her days. She gave him time for trips to Tulsa. He gave her time to work with the dogs and to do her job as a translator.

Thursday morning he took Tori to the apartment. Abby, the newest resident of Mercy Ranch, opened the door. Abby's eye had healed, the swelling had gone down and the bruises had faded. But she still wore the wary look of a woman who had been badly beaten.

"Eve's at the stable," she told him.

"Oh, okay." He shifted Tori to his left side. "I'll go down there to talk to her."

She smiled at him then, a half gesture that brought a brighter light to her gray-blue eyes.

"Give her time. That's all. Just time." She shrugged. "Do you want me to watch the little one? I'm not doing anything. Jack is a big believer in time. And I seem to have a lot of it on my hands these days. Other than an appointment with Kylie this afternoon, I'm at loose ends."

Leave Tori with a woman who was basically a stranger? He wasn't sure about that.

"I can take her up to the house where Jack and Maria are, if that helps. I can watch her there, under close supervision." She laughed a little. "I'm not saying you should blindly hand a child over to a stranger. I do understand that you don't know me very well."

"If you would go up to the house, I'd appreciate it if you would watch her. She has bottles, food and toys in her bag."

Abby took Tori from him and held her close. "Oh, you are a sweetheart. No wonder everyone on this ranch loves you."

"Thank you for watching her."

"No problem." She stepped out the door and closed it behind her. "I told Maria I'd help her with tonight's dinner. I have to do something. Watching Tori and cooking will keep me sane."

They walked together until the sidewalk forked toward the house and the stables. Ethan watched Abby as she entered the house. Once they were safely inside, he headed in the direction of the stable. In the distance he could see men moving a small herd of cattle toward a dry lot near an older barn. A cow broke free from the herd and one of the men brought her back, whooping so loudly Ethan could hear them even from a distance.

Farther off he could hear the steady drone of a tractor. He guessed someone was trying to cut grass while the weather was decent. Cutting grass was like washing a car—it never failed to rain afterward. Hopefully Jack's crew could get the hay baled before the rains forecasted for the weekend.

He walked through the open doors of the stable and stopped. Eve's horse was cross-tied in the middle aisle. He liked the setup for Jack's stable. Stalls on one side, office, take and feed on the other side, as well as open windows that looked out over the attached indoor arena.

Eve appeared, holding a bucket with brushes. She spotted him and stopped. "Where's Tori?"

"Abby took her to the main house to watch her. She said she thought we would be more comfortable with Jack and Maria overseeing her."

"I've spent time with her. She's a good person." She set the bucket on the ground and pulled out a comb.

Ethan watched as she eased up to Twister, patting him and talking to him as she started to comb his tail. He remained to the side, easily viewable by the horse but out of the way.

Eve moved efficiently and with practiced ease, combing the horse, then brushing. He even allowed her to check his hooves. But it was Eve who impressed him, not the horse. Eve with her dark hair pulled up in a bun with a few strands hanging loose. Eve with her dark eyes and expressive mouth.

"I wanted to apologize," he told her. "I overstepped. I took control and made decisions for you without discussing them with you first. That was wrong of me."

She untied the horse and led the animal to his stall, turning him back in and then closing the stall door. Twister leaned over, waiting for a rub of affection on his jaw. She gave it to him, leaning close to kiss his nose and tell him in a soft whisper that he was the best.

He was jealous of a horse. It stung, that realization.

"You're forgiven," she said as she backed away from the stall and turned to face him. "Please sit down. I hate getting a crick in my neck."

He sat on a nearby stool. "Better?"

"Yeah, better. You don't need to apologize, I do. This is more about me than it is about you. That's what I'm starting to realize. I've spent four years trying to control everything around me. You're not doing anything that any other man wouldn't do. It's my reaction to the situations that are out of control. It was just easier to blame you."

She gave him a rueful look and he grinned. "I'm glad to hear that. But still, I messed up."

"Oh, you did." She moved a little closer and he saw dark smudges under her eyes, a sign she hadn't been sleeping well. "I have a life here, Ethan. This life makes me feel safe. Whole. And then all of a sudden here you are with Tori and everything is thrown into chaos. There are going to be changes, neither of us can avoid that reality. But I can't handle this many changes. I think that's why I had the panic attack. It's just so much all at once."

"I know. And so here I go with another layer, and I hope you understand that this is beyond my control." He pulled out the letter he'd gotten from his lawyer. "I got this the other day and I need to share it with you. Basically it tells us we need a plan before we go before the judge. If we can't convince him we are going to give her a stable environment, he might very well put her in a foster home until we convince him we're suitable parents."

"What do we tell a judge to convince him we love her and we will give her a stable and loving home?"

"I don't know. But we have until the middle of June. The problem is, I can't stay. The dealership here is on schedule and I have good people who'll get it finished. My parents need my help at home."

"So you're leaving?" She seemed shocked by that. Had she thought he would stay forever?

"I am."

"What about the house you bought?"

"I'm keeping it for now. I need a place to live when I'm here because I can't expect Jack to give me a room on the ranch indefinitely. Eve, we have Tori. I know you didn't plan on raising a child but what are we going to do, abandon her to the system and let her take her chances?"

Her face paled. "Ethan, no. That isn't at all what I want. When you showed up here, I was shocked. But I can do this. I can be the person she needs. It wasn't what I planned. It wasn't what either of us planned. But I won't let her go."

"Then what's our plan? What do we tell the judge?"

She toyed with the lead rope she still held. "I wish I knew the answer to that. How do we convince a judge that we're the best option for a six-month-old little girl? What if he sees me as a detriment to raising her?"

"You're not a detriment. But as for the plan, I know what I want to tell him."

Her gaze dropped to the ground and he found it hard not to pull her close and hug her. He wanted to reassure her that they could do this. Together. But he'd learned his lesson the day he'd taken her to the house, wanting to surprise her.

She coiled the lead rope in her hand and lifted her gaze to meet his. Her eyes were soft, sad and her expression apologetic. "I think we tell him that we're committed to raising her together. We share custody, both of us equally invested in her upbringing and her life. Explain that James and Hanna named us as guardians, we're not married, but we love this little girl."

It wasn't what he wanted and he was sure it wasn't what a judge would want to hear. But it was all they had.

"I'll write that down and give it to my lawyer. I'll tell him that I've bought a house thirty minutes from Mercy Ranch so that we can be in the same area and work together on a schedule that will give her stability."

"It doesn't sound like enough."

"It'll have to be." He wanted to say more. But the time wasn't right. "I'm going to leave in the morning. I'm taking Tori with me."

Her eyes closed briefly but she nodded, agreeing with the plan.

"It's better that she ride to Texas with you," she conceded. "I'll drive down in the next week or two but it would be difficult for me to do that with Tori."

"I understand."

"When I come into that courtroom, is he going to see this chair and think that I can't handle being a mother to that little girl? Will he see a disability and ignore my abilities?"

"No, because I won't let him. No matter what, we're in this together. Right?"

"Right. Together."

He stood. "I'll bring Tori to you this afternoon so you can spend time with her before we leave."

"Thank you." She reached for his hand. "We are not going to lose her."

"I hope not. The last thing I want is for a judge to give custody to strangers."

He pulled his hand from hers. He had to walk away or he was going to do or say something that he shouldn't.

That was the last thing they both needed right now.

Twenty-four hours after their conversation, Eve found herself alone with her dogs. April, mom of the latest litter of puppies, sat next to her as Eve played with the puppies, socializing them, naming them, loving and crying over them. Soon they would go to individuals on the ranch and in the community who would commit to working with them for the next year. It was a long process and she would miss the puppies. But in the end they would be ready for homes where they would make a difference in the lives of their owners.

Tex had been one of those dogs. Unfortunately he'd failed the program. She'd gotten used to the fact that not all of her dogs would make it as service animals. But Tex, with time in her care and her home, would grow. He'd failed the program but he was exactly what Eve needed. He knew basic tasks and commands. More than anything, he was her friend.

"What's up?"

Eve smiled at Kylie. She wasn't surprised to see her friend lurking around.

"Oh, nothing. What's up with you?" Eve asked. She

bent down to scoop up a puppy and put it in the kennel. When she pointed, April went back in the fenced-in area. The rest of the puppies followed.

"You've had a tough week," Kylie said. "First with Tori being sick. And then Ethan and Tori left."

Eve smiled. When she decided to get involved, Kylie wasn't one to give up. Eve knew she'd keep asking little questions until Eve caved.

"Yes, I've had a tough week. But I'm surviving it."

"I know you are." Kylie sat down on the bench.

Eve backed up and spun her chair to face her friend. "I'm okay. Really."

Kylie pulled a tissue out of her purse and held it out.

"What's this for?" Eve asked, even as she took the tissue. Just in case. "You think I should cry?"

"No, I don't think you have to cry. Are you going to cry?"

"I'm good. Would you stop trying to make me cry? He's gone but I'm heading down next week. I'll stay with my parents until the court date."

"You're going alone?" Kylie sounded shocked.

"I can do that, you know. It's less than ten hours."

"I know how far it is."

"It's a long drive, but I can do it."

"Keep telling yourself that." Kylie smiled as she said it. "Glory said she'd go with you."

"I might take her up on that. I know I can do this but I'll admit to you and no one else, I'm scared. Last week Ethan decided to surprise me. He bought a house, a handicap-accessible house, about thirty miles from here. He didn't ask. He didn't plan this with me. He made a decision, thinking I should just accept it."

Kylie's eyes widened. "Uh-oh."

"And instead of being excited, I had a panic attack. My chair was in the back of his truck and he was planning our future and the only thing I could think of was, 'I'm stuck with no way to get out, no way to escape,' and it scared me. I live *here*. *This* is my home and my life."

Kylie didn't respond. Eve waited a full minute, wanting her friend to say something, to agree with her, to commiserate. Nothing happened.

"Say something," Eve prodded.

"No way."

"Kylie, I need for you to say something."

Kylie laughed. "No, you want me to agree with you that he did something horrible. And maybe he was wrong. A ranch is an awfully big thing to surprise someone with. And the assumption that you should live there with him. I'm guessing this was a bad attempt at a proposal?"

"Yes." She buried her face in her hands. "Oh, wow. He was proposing and I turned into a hot mess right there in his truck."

"Do you want my real thoughts on the matter?"

Eve uncovered her eyes and nodded. "Yeah, go for it."

"Mercy Ranch is safe. It's a known and you're afraid of the unknown. Everyone knows you here. You go to the same places every week, talk to the same people and you feel safe. But sometimes life isn't safe. When we step out of the boat and take chances, life can be messy, it can be frightening, and we can't control every situation."

Eve looked up at the clear blue sky. It was late May

now and the weather had warmed considerably. Bees covered the lawn, going from clover to clover. She turned her attention to the green fields where cattle and horses grazed. It had been a good spring, plenty of rain, the temperatures hadn't gotten too hot too soon.

She thought about Texas and suddenly, for the first time in a long time, she missed it. She missed her parents, overwhelming as they might be.

"For all my talk of being strong and independent, I've hidden myself away on this ranch."

"I wouldn't say you've hidden yourself away." Kylie reached for a puppy. "Okay, maybe a little. But maybe you needed this place and the safety net it provided. No one can tell you when to leave the safety of Mercy Ranch. You know more about how you feel than anyone else. I do think maybe it's time to consider the possibility of leaving. If not permanently, at least take this journey to Texas and see what happens."

"What if the judge doesn't give us custody?"

Kylie's expression softened. "I don't see how he couldn't. But I also don't know the mind of a judge. I know the goal would definitely be a loving, stable home environment with people who love and care for Tori."

"I'm the holdout," Eve said after a few minutes. "Because I don't know if I can be the person Ethan expects me to be. I loved him once. I think I still love him. But his need to make decisions for me is infuriating. And it isn't something new. I think if we'd gotten married, I would have resented that and it would have hurt our relationship."

"The thing I've learned about marriage is that we do things to irritate each other. There are habits, personality traits and moments that can either break us or cause us to grow. If you want a relationship that lasts, one that endures those moments, you learn to communicate."

"If we're going to raise Tori together, he has to learn that I am fully capable of making my own decisions. I know what is safe and what isn't. I know what I want and I don't want him to decide that for me."

"Tell him, not me," Kylie said as she put the puppy back in the kennel. "I'll take that one to raise."

"Because I know which one that is? You'll have to remember." Eve switched the conversation back to Ethan. "If we get joint custody of Tori, will it be okay to stay here until I can find a place of my own?"

Kylie rolled her eyes, clearly exasperated. "Of course you can stay here. You don't have to find another place to live, Eve."

"Maybe not right away, but I think it's time. I have used this as my safety net. But I think Tori and I need a place of our own."

"What about Ethan?"

Good question. Eve shrugged. "We'll work it out. He bought that ranch so he can be close to Hope and close to Tulsa. Life has a way of changing things up on us. This isn't what I expected but it feels right and I think God has been preparing me, getting me ready for the next step of my journey."

Kylie leaned down and hugged her. "I'm so glad we're friends."

"Me, too, more than I can say. And if you don't mind, I'll borrow Glory. If she doesn't mind being away from Cara."

"She offered, so I would take her up on it. She'll keep you entertained and the drive won't be so boring."

"Will she get Cara back?"

Kylie's eyes filled with tears. "Yes, she will. And that's the way it should be. We're hoping she can start classes and get her teaching degree. We'll help her as much as we can."

"They both need you, Kylie."

"I think we need them, too."

They put the rest of the puppies back in the kennel and started toward the house. There was an emptiness here now, with Ethan and Tori gone. She'd been so happy here before they came, before she realized how much she'd missed Ethan and before she knew the sweetness of Tori.

It seemed as if there shouldn't be a problem, as if this, as if they were meant to be. If she was a person looking at her life from the distance she would see only blessings and no obstacles. But the obstacle was hers and it was hidden and painful.

She loved Ethan. She had always loved him. But nothing had changed. She wanted to be cared for, not taken care of.

She didn't want to be his problem to solve.

Chapter Fifteen

The lawyer's office was paneled, lit only with lamps and smelled of lemon oil. The only magazines were either outdoors magazines or entertainment gossip magazines. Ethan hadn't come here to read.

But he had expected Eve to at least show up. He'd called and they'd talked for five minutes, going over the meeting with the lawyer and the court date and time. She'd agreed that they would present a united front.

And yet, she hadn't shown.

The lawyer, Guy Channing, came to the inner door and motioned him to follow. Ethan glanced out the window and didn't see Eve. He followed Guy down a darkly paneled hallway to an office that fit the rest of the building. Dark paneling, bookcases, a heavy oak desk. Guy sat behind the desk. Ethan took a seat in one of the leather-upholstered chairs on the opposite side.

"How's Tori?" Guy asked. "Adjusting?"

Ethan's gaze landed on the photos on the wall, of Guy, his wife and their three children. A happy family.

"Yes, she is. I mean, she's six months old. As long

as she eats and smiles, I assume she's happy. But if she isn't, if she's sad and wants her parents, how do I know? She can't exactly tell me." Ethan sat back, brushing a hand through his hair. The words had poured out of him, pushed by his fear for the future and for Tori. How was he supposed to know if she was happy?

"I'm sorry," Guy said. "I wish there were easy answers. She's young, I guess would be the best thing to say. She will grow up knowing she's loved. When she's older you'll tell her about her parents and how much they loved her."

"Right. I get that. But they're gone. And there are times I'm really angry that she doesn't have them. Instead she's stuck with me."

"And Eve Vincent?"

Ethan looked around, making his point.

"Maybe something happened." Benefit of the doubt. Nice.

"Yeah, maybe. But now I have to go before a judge and try to convince him that I can be a single dad. That I can raise Tori by myself."

"Is that what you want?" Guy asked. "I'm asking because we have to go before this judge on Monday and we have to convince him that you are a suitable guardian for this child. I have background checks, personal testimonies. But the judge is going to want to know that you want to do this and that you can do it. If you can't convince him, I'm afraid Tori will be taken into state custody."

"I can and will raise her. I want to raise her."

The lawyer turned to his computer. "Okay, then tell me the plan. You need to go in there with more than a simple, 'I can do this.' How can you do it? Do you have family support?"

"Yes, my parents and my sister, Bethany."

"Bethany suffers from depression." The lawyer didn't say it to pick a fight but it raised Ethan's hackles.

"Yes, she does. But she's in counseling and she has the right medication that she takes daily. She isn't raising the child. You asked if I have family support. I do."

"Ethan, I'm not trying to upset you. I'm going over all of the points of the case."

"Okay." Ethan took a deep breath. "Yes, I have family support."

"But you've decided to move and take the child out of state. What about support in your new home?"

"Eve Vincent lives less than thirty miles from my new home. I'm sure we will come up with a plan. I can also hire a nanny."

"You think Eve will agree to help?"

"I know she will."

Guy stopped typing. "Weren't you engaged to her at one point?"

"Yes, I was. She ended the relationship."

"Because?"

"She was in an accident in Afghanistan that left her paralyzed from the waist down. She didn't want to keep me in a relationship because she didn't want my pity or resentment."

"Ah."

Ethan was over this conversation and ready to move on. But his own words forced him to rethink things. Would he have pitied or resented Eve? He didn't think so. He couldn't imagine that ever happening. He admired her. He wanted to share a life with her.

He had really messed things up. Because he didn't pity her but she probably thought that he saw her as someone who needed to be taken care of. He probably had treated her like someone who needed to be taken care of. What he hadn't shown her was that he knew she was strong and independent. She could and had been taking care of herself without his help.

"Ethan, we need to get back on track." Guy spoke, drawing him back. "Any chance of reconciliation?"

"Probably not. If there was, I messed it up."

"Couldn't you unmess it up?"

Ethan laughed at that. "I'm not sure how."

The implication was to fix things for Tori. Ethan wanted more than a relationship based on guardianship. He wanted Eve in his life because she was the woman he loved.

But the truth was, she was in his life only because of Tori. If he hadn't gone looking for Eve, she never would have come back to Texas or back to him.

"I think we go with single-parent custody, but you have family support and you have the financial ability to hire a nanny or even a live-in housekeeper if necessary. Tori will not only be provided for financially but she will be loved and cared for. And that is what her parents wanted, and it is why they named you and Eve as guardians."

"That sounds good to me," Ethan agreed.

"I'll type this up. If you hear from Miss Vincent, please let me know. I can add to this if needed."

"If I hear from her, I'll let you know."

The lawyer stood. "Ethan, there is always hope."

Ethan agreed, there was always hope. All things work together for good for those who trust God.

As he walked out the front door of the building, he scanned the street, the parking lot. No sign of Eve. He was going to have to do a whole lot of trusting.

Eve was sitting on the side of the road with a car that had overheated, with no phone signal because they were in Nowhere, Texas, with nothing but fields for miles and miles. She glanced at her watch and groaned, because she'd missed the meeting. And she couldn't even call Ethan to tell him how sorry she was that she didn't make it.

Instead she found herself sitting on the shoulder of the road with Glory standing beside her. They waved as a car came over the horizon.

"Are you sure we should do this, Eve?" Glory asked for the fifth, maybe sixth time.

"Glory, do you have a better plan? We have to get help. I can't fix a leaking radiator. You've agreed that you have no hidden auto mechanic skills. We obviously can't walk all the way to town."

"Bluebonnet isn't too far, is it?"

"It's far enough that I don't feel like getting there on my own power." Eve drew in a breath, waiting, hoping. The car slowed when it saw them, then pulled to the shoulder of the road.

The driver got out, and Eve felt a silly grin break across her face.

"Eve Vincent? What in the world brings you back

to these parts?" It was Mrs. Carlson, Eve's freshman math teacher.

Small-town life did have its benefits. Knowing everyone in town could be a blessing when a person was stranded on the side of the road.

"Mrs. Carlson, I am so glad to see you."

The teacher laughed. "I bet you are. It's hot as blazes out here and you're a good distance from town."

"And there's no cell signal out here," Glory piped up. "Hi there, I'm Glory Blackwell."

"Glory, it is very nice to meet you. Where are you two headed?"

"To Bluebonnet," Eve acknowledged. "I have to meet with Guy Channing. I guess he recently moved his office from the capital."

"He certainly did. He was a state representative and decided he'd rather just do small-town law. He's a decent guy. How're your parents?" Mrs. Carlson asked as they headed back to her car.

"They're well. I'm staying with them for a week or two before returning to Oklahoma." Eve smiled at Glory, who opened the passenger door for her. After making the transfer, she quickly removed the wheels from her chair and Glory scooped it all up and stowed it in the trunk.

Mrs. Carlson got behind the wheel of the car and waited for Glory to climb in the backseat.

"Is that where you are now? Oklahoma? I've wondered."

"Yes, I've been living on Mercy Ranch."

"Oh, I've heard of it." Mrs. Carlson eased back onto the road. "It seems as if you're doing well."

It was a normal question and not the one she always feared. What had happened to her? Would she recover? She dreaded those questions.

"I am doing well, thank you." She smiled at her former teacher, a sweet woman with silver hair that hung straight to her shoulders and the kindest smile. That smile always made a kid, even a grown kid, feel accepted.

It didn't take long to reach Bluebonnet. On the drive, cell phone service returned, so Eve called her father and he told her he would pick her up in town and arrange a wrecker to take her car to the garage. She tried to call Ethan but he didn't answer.

"Here we are." Mrs. Carlson pulled into the parking lot next to the law office.

Home. Eve looked around the small town she'd grown up in. She'd forgotten how much she loved this place.

"Thank you for the ride. There isn't much traffic on that stretch of road. I'm not sure how long we would have waited." Eve remained in the seat as Glory got out to get her chair.

Moments like this were the ones that took adjusting to. She wanted to get out and take care of things herself. She didn't want to depend on someone else. As she sat there, Glory was getting her chair out of the trunk, putting the wheels back on. Eve laced her fingers together and forced herself to let it go.

"It isn't easy, is it?" Mrs. Carlson spoke, breaking the awkward silence.

"No, it isn't," Eve answered. "I want to get out and do this myself. But if I could do that, I wouldn't need the chair, would I? And I'm thankful for the help and the people in my life."

"I'm sure you are. Listen, Eve, I have to share this with you. I have MS. Multiple Sclerosis."

"I'm sorry. I didn't know."

Mrs. Carlson smiled. "Of course you didn't. I used to hide it very well. I didn't even tell the school administration, not until I had to. The day I couldn't feel my legs, I had to tell someone. I've learned to let people help me. I've also learned when to use whatever mobility aids I need. I see it as a way to preserve my energy for the other things I can do."

"You were always my favorite teacher for a reason." Eve hugged the other woman. "Thank you. I'm glad you were the one who happened by."

"So am I. There are a lot of coincidences in life. And then there are God moments that are meant to be. If you need anything at all, even if it's a sympathetic ear, you call me." Mrs. Carlson wrote her name on a scrap piece of paper. "I'm sure everything will work out for you. And when you're in town, give me a call and we'll have lunch at the café."

"I'll do that." Eve moved herself from the car to her chair. "Thank you."

"You're welcome. Talk to you soon. If you're in town for a few days, please come to church and see everyone."

"I will."

Glory started to push the chair. Eve stopped her. They'd had this discussion before. Glory was learning to push only when Eve asked for help. Or if she asked if Eve needed help.

They were at the door of the law office when it opened. The man who stepped out was on the early side of middle age with dark hair and a kind smile. He wasn't dressed in suit or tie but in jeans and a button-down shirt. But Eve pegged him as the lawyer.

"Mr. Channing, I'm Eve Vincent. And I'm obviously late. My car broke down and there was no cell service."

Mr. Channing glanced at his watch. "I'm sorry to hear that. And I'm more than sorry that I don't have a lot of time."

Eve groaned. "Great. And I'm sure Ethan thought I just didn't show up."

"That is what he thought. I'm sure you can explain. I'll give you a quick rundown. The judge is going to want to see that the two of you can give Tori a stable and loving home environment. He's going to want the two of you to show that you can work together and that you have a relationship that will allow you to do that. I'm hopeful but not too hopeful."

"What would give us the best chance of making sure the judge doesn't take her from us?"

He smiled at the question. "I think you know. But I don't want to see the two of you make a decision you can't live with that would possibly be more difficult for Tori when she gets older. The last thing I want is to meet up with you in a divorce or custody case."

"Of course. That's the last thing I want, too."

"Then I guess you'd better decide what is the first thing you want and what is the most important thing." He glanced at his watch a second time. "I'm sorry, I really do have to go. Ballet recital."

"Oh, I'm sorry for keeping you."

"I'm glad you were able to make it. Do you have a ride?"

"My dad is coming to get us." A car honked. "And there he is."

But when she turned, it wasn't her father. It was Ethan. She felt as if she lit up on the inside. It was a silly reaction. Just seeing a man shouldn't make everything better. But it did. And suddenly she wondered what she'd been so afraid of.

Communicate, Kylie had said. It sounded simple. Maybe it was simple and she'd made it difficult because she'd tried so hard to be independent. She'd been so afraid of being the person he took care of.

He parked and got out of the car. She waited for him, noticing that Glory slipped away, pretending to window-shop at one of the few stores in this part of town.

Ethan stepped onto the sidewalk, then he leaned against his car and looked at her. "You made it."

He didn't appear to be as happy to see her as she was to see him.

"I did. My car broke down. As a matter of fact, I see it now, on the way to the garage. Dad is coming to get me."

"How did you get to town?"

"Mrs. Carlson. And I talked to Mr. Channing, too." She breathed in, hoping for courage. "Ethan, I'm sorry. I'm sorry for hurting you four years ago. I'm sorry for the way I acted at the house. I know you're trying to do the right thing, and I keep messing things up. I realized that I've made my life safe. Then you came to town and made it uncomfortable. And you have this annoying habit of deciding what is best for me."

"I'm sorry, too. The house was a mistake. An expensive mistake." He grinned, and for a moment Eve's world felt right again.

"Trying to protect the people you care about isn't a mistake. Trying to do it without asking if they need protected, that's the mistake. By all means, if you see an asteroid falling right at this moment, do not stop to ask me if I need protecting."

They both laughed, and in the distance she heard Glory laughing. The kid was such an eavesdropper. They looked at each other and both smiled.

"Ethan, we can do this together, raising Tori. We can work on being better friends, on communicating. She needs us to be the adults she can count on."

"What do we tell the judge?" he asked.

"That we will both raise this child to the best of our ability. We will love her unconditionally. We will communicate and make sure we're both doing our best for her."

"I listed the house in Oklahoma. The real estate agent and I had discussed it before I left. I put it off until today. When you didn't show up for our appointment, I assumed that meant you weren't interested in shared custody."

"Oh."

He sighed. "We'll work this out."

He didn't smile. His eyes didn't flash with warmth. She got the terrible feeling that even though they could work things out for Tori's sake, Ethan was done with Eve.

She really didn't want him to be done with her.

Chapter Sixteen

Ethan walked up the steps of the courthouse with his parents, Bethany and Tori. Eve, Glory and Eve's parents were waiting inside for them. They'd talked again the previous day, meeting at the park to spend time together with Tori. Their plan was to present a united front.

But Ethan had other plans.

"You're here." Eve rolled forward, surprising him with an easy smile.

"You were worried?"

"Not at all," she said. "You clean up nice, Mr. Forester."

He grinned at her. He realized she hadn't seen him in a suit in a long time. Probably since a college dance they'd both attended. She cleaned up nice, too. She wore a dark blue dress and boots, and her hair was up in a bun. The messy kind that left tendrils of hair around her face. He thought she looked perfect for this day.

"We should go on up," Guy Channing said. He shook Ethan's hand and then Eve's. "Are the two of you ready?"

"As ready as we'll ever be." Eve put a hand to her stomach. "But nervous. Really nervous. What if…"

Guy stopped her with a raised hand. "I don't want to deal in what-ifs. My goal today is to make the three of you a family in the eyes of that judge. That is what we have here, correct?"

Ethan nodded. He looked to Eve. She inclined her head in response. He considered this moment but then let it go. They followed Guy to the elevator, and then down the hall to the courtroom. Their wait was minimal and soon they were called inside. The courtroom was a smaller family court. The judge sat at a desk on a dais behind a paneled wall. There were two tables. One for either side. In this case it was the state versus Ethan and Eve. An attorney for Tori, as well as a caseworker, was seated at the other table.

Ethan watched as their families took seats on the benches behind a short wall separating the court participants from those viewing the process.

The proceedings started and the judge studied the two of them as the lawyers for the state gave their side. Guy stood and gave their opening statement.

The questioning started, just as Guy had warned them. The judge asked questions. They were grilled by the guardian ad litem, hired by the state to defend Tori's rights and best interests.

They were promising Tori would spend time with both of them. Time split between homes.

The judge stopped speaking and glared at him.

"Mr. Forester, did you hear my question?"

"Yes, sir, you asked about living arrangements and Miss Vincent told you that we will each have our own place and that we will share custody of Tori. But that isn't really what either of us want." He looked at Eve. "Is that what you want?"

It was now or never. He'd tried to do this and he'd messed up. But this time he knew what he needed to say. And she would hopefully agree.

If she didn't, he would deal with the repercussions.

Eve considered the fact that maybe Ethan had lost his mind. He was standing in a courtroom, not really arguing with a judge but not really complying when the judge asked him if the proceedings could continue. If this continued, not only would they not get Tori, but she'd have to bail Ethan out of jail.

She implored him with her eyes to please sit.

Instead he glanced up at the judge. "Your Honor, can I speak?"

The judge sighed. "Please approach the bench."

Ethan went forward, smiling for all the world like a man having the time of his life. The judge leaned in and the two had a private conversation. The judge nodded and Ethan returned to the table where Eve sat with their dumbfounded attorney.

"Eve, I love you."

Eve wasn't surprised when he knelt in front of her. He was considerate that way, making sure they were eye to eye. She didn't know whether to be nervous or afraid, though. His expression was too serious, too thoughtful.

"Ethan, you're going to get arrested for disrupting a court proceeding." She looked to their attorney. "Is that a thing? Is this contempt of court?"

"I think we can come up with the bail money," Guy Chapman grinned.

She turned her attention back to Ethan. He smiled at her, and her heart took a strange leap. She considered cupping his cheeks with her hands and kissing them. Her gaze shot past him to the judge. The judge didn't look amused.

"Eve, let's do this right. Let's raise Tori as ours. Together. That's the way we're meant to be. I know you're afraid. I know you think I'll resent you or pity you. Maybe you think I deserve that dream we used to talk about when we were kids. But I want you, because life with you is my dream. I want you. We were supposed to say vows to one another, to have and to hold, better or worse, sickness or health. I want it all. I want the good times, the hard times and the blessings. With you. I can't promise that I won't ever do the wrong thing for the right reason. Or even the wrong reason. I can't promise you we won't fight. I think it's guaranteed we will. I can guarantee you that I'll love you forever." He pulled a ring out of his pocket. "I had this the other day and it didn't seem like the right time. Maybe I have a problem with timing." He glanced back at the judge and then smiled at her."

"Marry me, Eve. Be my wife. Be Tori's mom."

She kissed him. "I love you, too."

"Then please say yes," he whispered close to her ear, "or this will be very embarrassing."

"I would never embarrass you." She kissed him again, aware that around them conversation had broken out. The judge pounded his gavel on the desk. "I will definitely marry you."

"Mr. Channing, could you control your clients and please address the court as to the new developments?" the judge asked.

Guy stood. "Your Honor, I believe my clients would like to get married."

The judge stood. "We will recess for thirty minutes while they go downstairs for a marriage license. In thirty minutes, meet me outside at the fountain. No one should get married in a stuffy office when it's a perfect summer day outside."

Eve's mouth dropped. "What?"

"You just accepted my proposal," Ethan reminded her. "And I realize this looks like me taking control again, but I'm an optimist. Your mom has your birth certificate. We can have a marriage license and get married today. If you're willing."

She glanced around and realized that their families were smiling. The kind of smiles that said they were all prepared for this.

"Was the judge in on this?"

"Not at all. He's just a decent guy."

Eve backed away from the table. "Well, then, we should go get a marriage license."

An hour later Eve's mother placed a veil over her head and put a bouquet of wildflowers in her hands. "Ethan asked me to bring a veil. I found mine in the closet. I'm such a hoarder and for once it paid off."

Eve hugged her mom. "I'm so glad you're here."

"Me, too. I know he wasn't always my favorite. I wanted you to go to the Peace Corps, not the army. I wanted you to marry someone like your father. And maybe Ethan is more like your father than I realized. But I'm proud of you. We're proud of you."

"I love you, Mom."

Her mom dabbed at her eyes with a lace handkerchief

but then she seemed to recover and she pushed the scrap of lace into Eve's hand. "Oh, this is for you. Something borrowed and old. It was your grandmother's."

"Thank you." Eve took it, gently. "I think I might need this. Where are my flower girl and bridesmaid?"

"Glory and Tori are waiting outside in the hallway. They're ready when you are. Not that your flower girl can toss rose petals, but we did get her a little basket and she's holding it very nicely. Do you have regrets? This probably isn't the wedding you always thought it would be."

"It's the perfect wedding."

And it was. They stood next to a fountain with Glory and Tori on Eve's left, Guy Channing on Ethan's right. The judge smiled as he read the vows, ignoring Bethany, who had brought her camera for the occasion.

Their wedding guests were their families and the onlookers who stopped, curious and smiling as they realized they were witnessing a wedding.

"Ethan and Eve, I now pronounce you husband and wife. And lest you think I've forgotten our young Tori, I also pronounce you a family. I hope that you will love each other well and raise Tori to know she is loved. You may kiss the bride."

Ethan leaned. "May I?"

Eve put her arms around his neck and he lifted her from the chair and swung her in a full circle before kissing her. She held tight, wishing that the moment could go on forever. In the end, the crowds that had gathered began to clap.

Ethan kissed her once more, a sweet kiss, lingering for a moment with his forehead against hers. "I love you, Eve."

"I love you back, Ethan."

Epilogue

Tori toddled on the grass, Tex the chocolate Labra-doodle keeping a close eye on her. It was Tori's second birthday and she knew she was loved. Kylie held out her arms and Tori hurried to her side, sitting quickly, or perhaps falling, next to Cara, who was just four months younger.

The party had taken place at Mercy Ranch so that everyone could attend, including Jack. He sat nearby, his hand in Maria's as he watched all of his "children."

"Almost ready to go home?" Ethan asked, coming to sit next to Eve.

They'd kept the ranch house Ethan had bought. She'd made it her own and they even raised horses. But their path had taken a different direction. They trained horses for the disabled. They hosted a summer camp for a week each year, allowing disabled children to stay at the ranch, where they worked together on team building and they rode horses or went on hayrides.

"Are you okay?" Ethan asked.

She nodded but her hand went to her rounded belly.

"Eve?"

She let out the breath she'd held. "I think we need to go to the hospital."

"Contractions?" he said quietly. "Contractions!" That time he yelled. Everyone started staring. Her parents had been sitting in lawn chairs and they were on their feet.

"Be calm, it's just a baby. People have them every day. Ethan, stop. Do not pick me up."

He stepped back, dragging his hand through his hair. "We're going to have a baby."

"Are you going to pass out?" Kylie asked, coming to stand with them. "Because if so, you should sit and put your head down."

"I'm not going to pass out. I'm going to take my wife to Tulsa. Eve, are you sure? You weren't supposed to go into labor. They're doing a cesarean. It's scheduled for next week."

"Tell that to the baby," she teased. "Ethan, be calm. We're going to have a baby boy and it's going to be okay. We're going to be okay."

"Of course you are." Carson appeared at Ethan's side. "Can you drive or do I need to?"

"I can drive," Ethan said. "I'll take Eve if someone can bring Tori?"

"We've got her," Eve's mom spoke up. "She wants to go with her nana."

Tori heard the word *nana* and immediately ran to Eve's mom.

"Okay, everything is good. Ethan, we need to call Dr. Lambert."

"Right, call the doctor. Calling the doctor." He had his phone out and Eve left him there talking.

She managed to get about twenty feet in the direction of the truck before another contraction hit. Kylie held out a hand and Eve took it, holding a little too tight she thought. Kylie smiled through the pain.

When the contraction ended, Kylie took the handles of the chair and got her to the truck. Ethan caught up with them, and he was back to his calm-and-in-charge self. He picked up his wife, kissing her once before putting her in the truck.

"We're going to have a baby." He kissed her again.

"Right here in this truck if you don't hurry up."

He grinned but he closed the door and a minute later they were on their way to Tulsa.

Three hours later Ethan was holding Jack West Forester. Jack had dark hair, a lot of it. He had a red wrinkled face and good lungs, if the cry he'd given at birth meant anything.

"We're blessed," he told his wife.

She smiled, that smile that always turned his world upside down. "Could you please put that baby next to me?" she asked.

"I certainly can. And I'm going to get Tori. We need a moment, just the four of us before everyone else comes in and life changes completely."

"I agree. Go get her."

He found his daughter, Tori, in the waiting room with their families and their Mercy Ranch family. "Jack West Forester weighs seven pounds. He's pretty much perfect. And even if he isn't, you'll all say he is."

"Guaranteed," Sierra said. "They always lie and say that babies are cute. They aren't."

"Same old Sierra," Isaac West commented. "Try to move this along so we can see him for ourselves."

Ethan picked up Tori and she kissed his cheek. "Daddy."

"I love you, little girl."

"Love you."

They entered the room where Eve and Jack were waiting. Ethan didn't know a man could be this happy. It went beyond anything he'd ever expected or experienced.

Eve opened her eyes and smiled at them. "Tori, meet your baby brother."

"Jack," Tori said.

"Yes, Jack." Ethan sat on the stool next to the bed and placed Tori down next to Eve. It was the perfect moment. But then, their lives were made up of those moments. They were a family.

Ethan thought about the plans they'd made years ago when they'd been happy and in love, and he looked at the reality.

Even with its ups and downs, the reality was truly beautiful.

* * * * *

If you loved this story,
pick up the other books
in the Mercy Ranch series,

Reunited with the Rancher
The Rancher's Christmas Match

from bestselling author
Brenda Minton

And don't miss these other great books
in the miniseries Bluebonnet Springs

Second Chance Rancher
The Rancher's Christmas Bride
The Rancher's Secret Child

Available now from Love Inspired!
Find more great reads at www.LoveInspired.com

Dear Reader,

Thank you for joining me on this journey. I'm so blessed to get to do what I love for a publisher I love.

My editors at Love Inspired have always encouraged me and I appreciate the stories they've allowed me to tell. Some stories are easier than others. The goal is always a romance that readers believe in and maybe fall a little bit in love with. Every now and then a character like Eve Vincent will come along and challenge me to something more.

I loved writing this book in the Mercy Ranch series and I hope that you'll love Eve and Ethan!

Blessings,

Brenda Minton

COMING NEXT MONTH FROM
Love Inspired®

Available June 18, 2019

THE AMISH WIDOWER'S TWINS
Amish Spinster Club • by Jo Ann Brown

Leanna Wagler has barely gotten over Gabriel Miller standing her up and announcing he was marrying someone else when the widower and his twin babies move in next door. Now she's his temporary nanny, but can they finally reveal their secrets and become a forever family?

A LOVE FOR LIZZIE
by Tracey J. Lyons

When her father has a heart attack, Lizzie Miller's family needs help to keep their farm running, and her childhood friend, Paul Burkholder, volunteers. After a tragedy in the past, Lizzie withdrew from the community and Paul, but now she's finally dreaming of the future...and picturing herself by his side.

HEALING THE COWBOY'S HEART
Shepherd's Crossing • by Ruth Logan Herne

With his hands already full caring for his orphaned niece and nephew, cowboy Isaiah Woods finds a sick mare in foal. Now he must rely on the expertise of veterinarian Charlotte Fitzgerald to nurse the animal back to health, but will their business arrangement turn into something more?

WANDER CANYON COURTSHIP
Matrimony Valley • by Allie Pleiter

When his stepfather and her aunt get engaged, Chaz Walker and Yvonne Niles are sure it's a mistake. But will the surly cowboy and determined baker discover that the best recipe for love often includes the heart you least expect?

THE COWBOY'S FAITH
Three Sisters Ranch • by Danica Favorite

After being left at the altar, the last thing Nicole Bell wants is a reminder of her humiliation. But when Fernando Montoya—the brother of her former best friend who stole her fiancé—shows up, she can't avoid him...especially since he's the only person capable of helping her troubled horse.

HOMETOWN HOPE
by Laurel Blount

Five-year-old Jess Bradley hasn't spoken in the three years since her mother's death—until she begs her father, Hoyt Bradley, to stop a beloved bookstore from closing. Desperate to keep Jess talking, can Hoyt set aside a long-standing rivalry and work with Anna Delaney to save her floundering store?

Get 4 FREE REWARDS!

We'll send you 2 FREE Books plus 2 FREE Mystery Gifts.

Love Inspired® books feature contemporary inspirational romances with Christian characters facing the challenges of life and love.

FREE Value Over $20

SPECIAL EXCERPT FROM

HQN

Read on for a sneak peek at
the second heartwarming book in
Lee Tobin McClain's Safe Haven series,
Low Country Dreams!

Yasmin shifted on the glider, set it rocking with one foot and tucked the other foot up under her. The air was cooling now, a slight breeze bringing the fragrance of oleander flowers. It seemed only natural for Liam to shuffle closer on the glider. To let his arm curve around her shoulders.

Yasmin's breath whooshed out of her. Talking with Liam about her brother had made her feel vulnerable, but also relieved. Less alone. She remembered when she could share anything with Liam and he would always have her back. Such a wonderful feeling, especially after her brother had stopped being able to be that rock and that support to her.

Now Liam turned to meet her gaze head-on. His hand rose to brush back a curl that had escaped her ponytail. "I like your hairstyle," he said unexpectedly, his voice a tone deeper than usual. "Reminds me of the old days, when we were in school."

"In other words, I look like a kid?" Her words came out breathy, and she couldn't take her eyes off him.

Slowly, Liam shook his head. "Oh, no, Yasmin. You don't look like a kid at all." His eyes flickered down to her mouth, then back to her eyes.

Yasmin's heart fluttered like a terrified bird. Her stomach, her chest, all that was inside her felt squeezed by warm hands, melting.

How she wanted this. This opportunity to talk to Liam in a low, intimate voice. To feel that sense of promise, that there was something happy and bright in their future together.

She tried to grasp on to the reasons why this couldn't happen. How she didn't dare to have children, because the risk of them developing a mental illness was so high. Not only because of Josiah, although that was the main thing, of course. But also because of her mother's issues.

As if all of that wasn't enough, Yasmin knew she wasn't past the safe age herself. What if she got into a relationship and then started having delusions and hearing voices?

It was hard enough taking care of her brother, her blood relative. She owed him and bore the burden gladly. But she couldn't expect a romantic partner to do the same for her, wouldn't want someone to.

Wouldn't want Liam to.

If she let things go where they were headed right now, if she let him kiss her, she wasn't sure she would have the strength to push him away again. Doing it once had nearly killed her. Maybe she could be strong enough, but only if she put an end to this before getting closer. "I think we should go."

His head tilted to one side, his eyes steady on her. "Do you really think so?"

She hesitated, clung for just a moment to the possibility of not being the responsible one, the caretaker, the one who took charge of things and tried to make everything work out. She could let herself do what she wanted to do every now and then, couldn't she? She could be spontaneous, go with her emotions, her heart.

But no. Her duty was clear. Her life was about taking care of her family, not about indulging in something pleasurable for now, but ultimately dangerous to someone she cared about. Liam was too good of a man, had suffered too many of life's blows already, to be shackled with Yasmin's issues. "Yes," she said firmly. "I really think so."

Don't miss Lee Tobin McClain's
Low Country Dreams, *available June 2019*
wherever Harlequin® books and ebooks are sold.

www.Harlequin.com

PHLTMEXP0619

Love Inspired®

Inspirational Romance to
Warm Your Heart and Soul

Join our social communities to connect
with other readers who share your love!

Sign up for the Love Inspired newsletter
at **www.LoveInspired.com** to be the
first to find out about upcoming titles,
special promotions and exclusive content.

CONNECT WITH US AT:

Facebook.com/groups/HarlequinConnection

 Facebook.com/LoveInspiredBooks

 Twitter.com/LoveInspiredBks

LISOCIAL2018